Dear Reader,

Thank you for your interest in my book. I really appreciate your support. I hope you enjoy.

I grew up in Oxnard, California. When I was younger, I saw too many injustices unfold before my eyes and I did not know how to make sense of them. However, as I got older and conducted research of my own, I gained a deeper understanding of my lived experiences. For example, I learned that there are always multiple sides to each story, yet we are only told one side. Consequently, we take that side as the only truth. In this book, I tell the other side of stories—the side that is intentionally untold and unheard. It is very important to note that although some settings and characters in this book are fictional, the stories I tell are not only based on my observations, but grounded in research articles, government databases, books, reports, newspaper articles, and so on. If you have any doubt, do some research on your own.

I ask that you remain open-minded throughout the entire reading of this book. This does not mean you have to agree with me. Instead, I ask you to make an honest effort to try to understand me. Because I speak on issues through an entirely different viewpoint, you may feel uncomfortable, unsettled, or even angry during your reading of my stories. Rather than feeling personally attacked by my stories, I urge you to investigate and learn more about your own misconceptions. Why is it that my observations and analyses are drastically different than yours? Reach out to friends, co-workers, family, youth, community members, activists, educators, or whoever for different worldviews. The main purpose of this book is to create awareness and inspire conversations around social injustices not only in Oxnard, but also in other communities.

Siguiendo Adelante,
Martín Alberto Gonzalez

About the Author

Martín Alberto Gonzalez is a Xicano raised in Oxnard, CA. He completed his undergraduate studies at California State University, Northridge. Currently, he is a doctoral student in the Cultural Foundations of Education Department at Syracuse University, where he became the first Ford Foundation Predoctoral Fellow in the university's history. He is the youngest of seven, yet the only one in his family to go to a four-year university. Because he personally observed his older siblings and his community's talents and interests be denied and repressed via their schooling, he became interested in educational issues related to Latinx students.

21 Miles of Scenic Beauty...
and then Oxnard

Counterstories and Testimonies

by

Martín Alberto Gonzalez

Copyright © 2017 by Martín Alberto Gonzalez

First Printing: 2017

ISBN-13: 978-0692980453
ISBN-10: 0692980458

For speaking engagements, inquiries regarding current mailing address, or for any other questions regarding this book and its author, please contact:

vivaoxnard@gmail.com

To purchase this book please visit:

http://www.amazon.com/dp/0692980458

Note: The price of this book will remain relatively inexpensive in order to remain as accessible as possible. If you are unable to purchase a copy at listed price, please contact vivaoxnard@gmail.com directly for more information about getting a copy.

Acknowledgements

A few stories in this collection contain material that originally appeared elsewhere, and I thank those editors and publisher. This material has been reprinted with permission of the publisher. "Wasting talent: Using counter-storytelling to narrate dismal educational outcomes," Martín Alberto Gonzalez, *Journal of Latinos and Education*, July 2017, Taylor & Francis Ltd.

This book was put together with the help of three incredible, critical Women of Color. I owe a huge shout out to Camilla Josephine Bell for providing commentary, suggestions, and encouragement throughout the development of this book project. Likewise, aside from providing support and looking over earlier drafts, Dr. Aja Y. Martinez challenged me to write both descriptively and unapologetically. Lastly, I would like to give special thanks and much appreciation to Jessica Irene Ramirez for her support, compassion, patience, and thoughtful conversations about our experiences growing up in Oxnard.

As for logistics, I would like to thank the following people: Natalie Alejandra Delgado and Sophia Kardaras, for assisting me in designing the cover and editing other ideas related to this book project; Austin Lujan, OHS 2017 graduate, who drew the "Hope" wall I am featured in front of; Griselda De Los Reyes, an Oxnard-Native, for drawing the cover and making my thoughts come to fruition through her art; and, last but certainly not least, Jordan Beltran Gonzales for blessing me with his editing expertise. Thank you.

Para: Matt de la Peña,

You're an inspiration!

Enjoy!

For every negative story told,
there's always a positive
one... Be your own
Storyteller!

Con Amor,

Until the lions have their own historians, the history of the hunt will always glorify the hunter... Once I realized that, I had to be a writer. I had to be that historian. It's not one man's job. It's not one person's job. But it is something we have to do, so that the story of the hunt will also reflect the agony, the travail—the bravery, even, of the lions.

—Chinua Achebe

Contents

21 Miles of Scenic Beauty...
and then Oxnard

Nothing good ever comes out of Oxnard, California. That's what I've been told my whole life. This message has been said to me both directly and indirectly. Oxnard residents internalize it, too. Whenever I speak to people concerning what is beautiful about Oxnard, they tend to limit their list to the beach, the weather, The Collection, the uppity shopping plaza—along with its *boujee*, over-priced shops, restaurants, and bars—and Toppers Pizza. For the most part, everything else either goes completely unnoticed or is readily demonized and degraded.

Needless to say, Oxnard has a bad reputation. In fact, most people I talk to who are not from Oxnard, but know about it, usually avoid it entirely. A few frequent polite responses I have come across include, "I have passed by Oxnard before, on the freeway," "I know where it is, but I've only been to the Camarillo Outlets," and a more recent one, "Yeah, I have been to Oxnard, only The Collection, though," and to all three I always reply, "Foo, that ain't Oxnard!" with an exaggerated frown on my face.

For my people not familiar with Oxnard, let me contextualize the city my siblings and I grew up in. The population in Oxnard is roughly 200,000, comprised of Latinas/os/x, Whites, Asians (with a prevalence of Filipinos), and Blacks, although Latinas/os/x, specifically Mexicans, are everywhere and a great majority of the population. Oxnard is uniquely difficult to describe to others because it is neither city nor country, but rather characterized as something in between. To some, Oxnard is strictly an agricultural city, often referred to as the "home of the strawberries." When I tell people that I am from Oxnard, CA, many immediately associate it with agriculture. Oxnard is filled with agricultural workers as a result of the Bracero program in the 1950s that brought Mexicans into the U.S. solely for their 'arms' and labor.

Due to its geographical location and demographic composition of undocumented residents, Oxnard has become an extremely successful agricultural site. Sitting on the Pacific Ocean coast about an hour south of Santa Barbara and an hour north of Los Angeles, it has ideal harvesting conditions. That said, many of the field workers are undocumented with very little autonomy and limited options in terms of occupations because of their undocumented status. Coincidentally and yet not surprisingly, nearby high schools do not appear to equip students with the appropriate skills and requisites for higher education, and it seems as if Students of Color (documented or not) face similar, though arguably less harsh predicaments such as constrained mobility as the undocumented field workers who they pass every morning before going to school.

Unfortunately, the overabundance of undereducated *Raza* with very little opportunities has created a negative reputation. Even people from Oxnard think it's bad. Oxnard's reputation is epitomized by an incredibly depressing meme from *The Lion King*, in which Simba asks Mufasa, "What about that shadowy place?" and Mufasa responds, "That's Oxnard, you must never go there." The Instagram (IG) page "StayClassyOxnard" further preserves Oxnard's negative, inhumane reputation by posting images of Oxnard folk going about their daily lives working with the scraps they were given. Many of the pictures featured on this IG page are either homeless or seemingly *Raza gente* acting or dressing ridiculously. Without knowing anything else, people outside of Oxnard receive only these images and stories.

3

Regardless of its seemingly "bad" reputation, Oxnard is beautiful. And not only in the traditional sense of beauty. In other words, I am not referring to commonly known parts of Oxnard that are readily deemed beautiful such as the multimillion dollar homes near the harbor and beach or even The Collection, along with its patio-dog-feeding restaurants. I am talking about the side of Oxnard that is often talked about in a negative light. The side that some people call the "ghetto" part of Oxnard. That is, the beautiful Brown people. The "homies"—both skinny and big, in 2XL, T-Shirt Warehouse-brand plain tees, oversized Dickies shorts, and long white socks. The South Side down Bard near Squires. The fiercely avoided *La Colonia* community. The *chamoy*-ridden swap meet at Oxnard College on weekends. The overcrowded parks filled with *Raza* cooking some *carne asada* and playing sloppy soccer with jeans and sandals. The tuba bumping *banda musica y sombrero*-wearing *paisanos* at Ruby's on a weekend night. In my opinion, these and many more are what make Oxnard beautiful. Yet, current representations of Oxnard tell us otherwise.

Truth be told, we easily encounter subliminal messages suggesting that Oxnard is not beautiful. If you take the Pacific Coast Highway (aka the PCH) from Los Angeles/Santa Monica to Oxnard, you'll eventually pass Malibu. As you enter Malibu, you will come across a sign that states, "Malibu…21 Miles of Scenic Beauty." Many tourists either drive slowly and mess up the traffic flow or park and get out of their car to take a picture in front of this sign. Needless to say, after the "21 Miles," the beauty "ends," even though Oxnard is the next city over and also has a beach. This explains why very few tourists and visitors dare to continue northbound past Malibu into south Oxnard. The reputation and people there are seemingly too "dangerous" and "out of control" for *innocent*, well-to-do visitors.

Because of this, I always visualize a "...and then Oxnard" after the "21 Miles of Scenic Beauty" to poke fun at the fact that Oxnard, for the most part, is seen as "bad" and undesirable, especially as it's juxtaposed with neighboring communities. While certain aspects of Oxnard such as the beach and the recently built, high-end restaurants are glamorized and sought out, everything else including all the beautiful Brown people who keep the city running, along with all their unique ways of living and being, fall by the wayside and are badly talked about. Hopefully, Oxnard residents and visitors will eventually appreciate all of what makes Oxnard what it is—unconditional and all-encompassing beauty.

Boxnard

Whether we know it or not, boxing runs in the blood of *la gente de* Oxnard. Whenever I tell people that I am from Oxnard, some outsiders make an immediate association with boxing. In fact, to boxing fanatics, Oxnard, better yet Boxnard, is known as the epicenter of boxing, where then and current professional boxers such as Fernando "Ferocious" Vargas, Brandon "Bam Bam" Ríos, Mikey Garcia, Victor

"Vicious" Ortiz, or Hugo "The Boss" Centeno Jr. have trained at the La Colonia Youth Boxing Club or at the Robert García Boxing Academy, named after a notable professional boxer and current professional trainer. Because it was everywhere growing up, boxing as a sport grew on me and I familiarized myself with various boxing techniques and strategies. While I was never directly involved with boxing, the boxing culture was and continues to be prevalent in my city. Even today, whenever I go home, I see youngsters and older folks sparring at beat-up community recreational centers, gyms, and Boys and Girls Clubs.

By far, one of the best-known boxing tactics is a counterpunch. To a casual observer, a counterpunch may appear to be simply a punch that is thrown immediately after an attack launched by an out-of-control, aggressive opponent. It is that and nothing more. However, a religious boxing follower will disagree and argue that counterpunchers are far beyond tactical. As fierce opportunists, boxers rely heavily on mistakes by their opponents with the goal of not only accumulating points on their scorecards, but ultimately a chance at a knockout. Thus, in this sense, a counterpunch becomes an important, potentially match-ending tactic. After all, some of the best knockouts ever witnessed in boxing history have resulted because of counterpunches.

Aside from the fact that I have met many people from Oxnard who are fighters, both literally and figuratively, I have been able to make a connection between counterpunches in the sport of boxing and Oxnard's reputation. *La Raza de*

Oxnard are constantly in a fight. However, unlike an ordinary boxing match that takes place in a ring or in a run-down alley, this fight takes place in an entirely different realm—that is, through stories. Every day, negative stories are told about Oxnard, especially its *Raza*.

These stories are violent and misleading—they have established a dominant narrative that overrides and taints the reputation of Oxnard with a solemn undertone of despair. This taken-as-truth narrative says that almost everything from Oxnard is "bad" and up to no good. Regardless of whether they are misleading, these persuasive stories become real and believable since they are told by both people in power such as politicians, journalists, teachers, researchers, etc. and by people without power who have internalized the negativity.

To make matters worse, the news and newspapers supplement this narrative with endless stories that perpetuate the idea that Oxnard, along with its people, is extremely dangerous. This dominant narrative misrepresents and silences anything positive that comes out of Oxnard. This is exactly why Oxnard's reputation is bombarded with stories about shootings and stabbings. Yet we rarely hear stories about people who are excelling and doing well, such as Oxnard-born Mexican professors who are doing groundbreaking research at the best universities in the U.S. Which is true, by the way.

This is where counterpunches come in. Figuratively speaking, we can punch back. We can disrupt this often-told negative narrative about Oxnard through counterstories. To be exact, counterstories are stories seldom heard that challenge detrimental and inaccurate dominant stories about marginalized and often misrepresented communities and people of color. Similar to counterpunches in boxing, counterstories serve as way to debunk, annihilate, or "knock out" misrepresentations of communities of color. To be sure, counterstories continue engaging in stories that are told about us, without us. The conversations and stories do not stop there, nor could we ever argue that it will ever stop. Yet, our counterpunches can create change not only in how others think about us, but more importantly how we think about ourselves.

When teaching others about counterstories, I reference a provocative report published in 2006 by Tara Yosso and Daniel Solórzano, "Leaks in the Chicana and Chicano Educational Pipeline," which provides a chart that illustrates the poor educational outcomes of Chicana/o students beginning in elementary school and continuing to high school, community college, and four-year universities. Immediately, the numbers are telling—Chicana/o students "lag" academically behind other racial and ethnic groups. On one hand, this chart could be interpreted as Chicana/o children and parents not valuing or caring about their education. Similarly, some people use this chart to verify their assumptions that Chicana/o students are inherently unintelligent. Unfortunately, I often hear this jargon used to describe why people like me do not do well in education. These are "dominant" and played-out stories. With respect to boxing, these explanations and stories are attacks launched by an out-of-control, aggressive opponent, namely people who are unwilling to see the next generation of Brown, proud youth and adults succeed.

On the other hand, for others like myself, this chart tells a completely different story. This points to injustices such as under-resourced schools, culturally irrelevant curriculum, underprepared teachers, and/or congested classrooms as prominent reasons in explaining educational disparities between Chicanas/os and other students. Again, in terms of boxing, these explanations and stories are counterstories or "counterpunches." The aforementioned example of the ambiguous yet telling educational outcomes of Chicana/o students sheds light on the importance of counterstories or "counterpunches." Without both sides of a story, we make the mistake in believing that there is no other explanation.

For a long time, I accepted all stories told about my Oxnard community and me as common, taken-for-granted knowledge and truth. In recent years, though, I realized that almost all the stories told about my community, my family, and me are told in a bad light with very little validity. Everything about my community and me —how we dressed, looked, and talked—was negative and had to be corrected. The stories I heard growing up told only one side of the story and were neither critical nor fully analytical. In turn, I realized the need to construct more stories—our own stories—to help debunk false images and ensure that an alternative depiction is portrayed and distributed. The stories in this book are examples of counterpunches as counterstories. However, it is important to note that counterstories come in all shapes and forms—films, poetry, theatre, dance, drawings, books, oral stories, and more.

We need stories in which we actually have a say in how we want to be presented and represented. Stories that give people, especially those who believe in everything they read and see, a true sense of those perspectives rarely told through a first-hand experience. These stories we tell are very important because they will serve as valuable tools to deconstruct negative and false portrayals presented in dominant stories about our community. Rather, they will allow us to construct and establish empowering stories that make you feel good about who you are and where you come from. In this way, I, like many others aware of the damaging stories told about us, will keep "swinging" by telling stories of my own in hopes that I continue to land counterpunches.

*This piece was inspired by and references a counterstorytelling framework originally published in "Critical Race Methodology: Counter-Storytelling as an Analytical Framework for Education Research," by Daniel G. Solórzano and Tara J. Yosso.

Mucha Crema a los Tacos

Mucha crema a los tacos is by far one of the most frequent phrases we use as a family. In English, it literary translates to "put too much sauce on your tacos." However, like most of our phrases, the true meaning gets lost in translation. Depending on who you talk to, *mucha crema a los tacos* can mean a variety of things. In its simplest form, it means don't exaggerate. If translated to similar, commonly used phrases in English, some people may compare it to "don't toot your own horn so much," "don't stretch the truth," or "don't get carried away." I am sure we all know a lot of *gente* who put *mucha crema a sus tacos.* For the sake of word count, I won't make a list. But you know who you are.

I come from a family of oral storytelling. For the most part, everyone in my family likes to tell stories in their own unique way. This is partly why we use the phrase so much. If my family and I were *taqueros,* we would be best known for putting *mucha crema a nuestros tacos.* We drown our stories in details, so whenever someone throws in an exact amount or a specific detail, one of us immediately jumps in and asks, "Ok. Now tell us without all the *crema*?" Occasionally, this forces us to change the details in our stories, but most of the time, the excessive *crema* remains.

Recently, I questioned why my relatives and close friends put *mucha crema a sus tacos.* I have come to the conclusion that it is because they are so invested in keeping their stories interesting, and I don't blame them. The *crema* works. Like *tajín y límon* on *pepinos*, the overabundance of *crema* in stories makes them that much more tasteful. Stories wouldn't be the same without it. Because of my experiences with *taquero* storytellers who put *mucha crema as sus tacos*, I am a firm believer that even the most exaggerated, Oscar-winning stories are meaningful in one way or another. Just because the details in the story seem extremely excessive does not mean that we should discount the story entirely.

Depending on the context and situation, I think we should entertain every single story—no matter how ridiculous it sounds. People remember and tell stories around what stood out to them and from their own unique vantage points, so these stories take on a different meaning and intention. After all, it is nearly impossible to recall from memory every exact detail of what happened. Many of you will read the stories in this book and immediately think that I, too, put *mucha crema a mis tacos*. Don't get it twisted, though. Underneath all the layers of *crema* in my stories, there is always a hint of truth.

who are on top at the expense of others do nothing to prevent it or stop it. You know, the type that produces socially unjust outcomes and then directs blame at those who are already at the bottom for their lack of effort.

One hot summer day, my partner Jessi pointed this out to me. She had just completed her first Chican@ Studies course ever at CSUN, the epicenter of Chican@ Studies. Fresh off her first year in college, to her, everything was wrong with the world. Oppression this. Sexism that. Jessi was that type. Problematic was her favorite word. A fun-ridden trip to a festival would boil down to patriarchy and deconstructing normative ways of thinking about gender. I knew I could not go to Disneyland with her because all she would do is complain about how princesses reaffirm the idea that women should not be leaders and that they should be complacent and wait for their husbands to save them.

Anyways, *la playa* became our safe haven during the summer because both of us lived as students in the San Fernando Valley throughout the year. Without a beach in sight as college students, we made it our priority to go to the beach as much as we could while we were home to make up for blistering hot days spent in the valley. One summer, Jessi and I went to the beach almost every single day. Everyday exposure to practices and norms of *la playa* opened a door for Jessi to analyze the social injustices taking place. I swear she was more wary and observant than a trained sociologist. Without a pen and paper, she would make observations and then bring them to light in order to start conversations about them. She would constantly exclaim to me, "Dang, you are so oblivious!" whenever I did not catch someone being "racist" or "offensive."

On an ordinary hot summer day in Oxnard, Jessi and I went to the beach for a run. Gasping for air, we stopped to sit down on the rocks that separate the beach from the harbor. A perfect view of both the harbor and the beach—or so I had thought. Right before I began to meditate and think about how blessed I was to grow up in a city so close to *la playa,* Jessi abruptly said, "Look! Can you believe it?!"

Not knowing exactly what she was talking about, I quickly agreed, "I know! We are very blessed to live by this beautiful *playa.*"

But Jessi looked at me as if I had just stepped on her brand new white shoes. She smirked, "No foo, I am talking about how messed up this *playa* is! Everyone at the kiddie beach is Brown, *La Raza,* and everyone at Silver Strand is White! Ain't that messed up?"

I made a quick observation to accompany the frown on my face. "How?" I told her, "they are just trying enjoy their time at the beach. I don't see anything wrong with that."

She shoved me gently. "Open your eyes for once, Martín! I thought you took Dr. Tracy Buenavista's Critical Race Theory course at CSUN?"

She continued animatedly, "It's rarely natural that people separate themselves based on race, it is usually some government scheme. Divide and conquer! At the end of the

17

day, *La Raza* is negatively impacted, while the whites remain on top. Don't you see it?" She asked impatiently.

Knowing that she was going to continue her racism tangent, I interjected, "C'mon! Here we go again. Every single time! You took one ethnic studies class and now you know everything."

"I'm serious!" she exclaimed, to which I questioned, "So how exactly is this messed up again?"

"First of all," she said, "let's start off with the name itself. 'Kiddie beach'? 'Kiddie,' really?" She continued in a loud, sarcastic voice, "I am a grown ass person, those are grown ass people, I take care of my damn self, don't be 'kiddie-ing' me as if I am incompetent or as if need to be supervised like some type of animal or savage. Let me guess, *those* people are uncivilized."

"Really, Jessi? You're trippin'!" I replied while I shook my head. "They call it 'Kiddie Beach' because parents tend take their kids there since that is where the harbor and beach meet and there happens to be no waves, thus 'safer.' The people there happen to be Brown. That's all. Nothing more, nothing less."

"See there's another problem," she protested immediately. "What are they trying to say? Is it that all *La Raza* does is make babies? What's next? That they make babies purposefully to take advantage of the welfare system and use up all their food stamps on all those chips and Kool-Aid jammers they are enjoying at this 'kiddie' beach?" Jessi raised her eyebrows as she made a duck lips.

"Jessi, you are overanalyzing this whole thing. Just enjoy the—"

"The view?" She interrupted, "Oh you mean the fact that this 'white' beach has beautiful, eye-opening eight to ten feet seemingly crystal clear waves, while this Brown 'kiddie' beach has toxic wastes trailing from all these fishing boats that are in and out of the harbor? It's called environmental racism. Look it up!"

She had a point. I stared at her thinking about what she said. And I was silent.

She continued without skipping a beat, "You know I don't mess with oceanography or whatever that's called, but I do know that those waves are more than just to surf on or get knocked over with. They also filter the water. With the 'Kiddie Beach,' the science is easy, no waves, no filter! So all the toxins and nasty chemicals or whatchamacallit are funneled in and aren't funneled out since there aren't any waves. The toxins are concentrated in this little area of water. That's really harmful. It is kind of like concentrated poverty. You get it?"

I laughed, "You had to go there, huh?"

"What?" She stared at me with a no-you-didn't face. "You think I am lying?" She continued aggressively, "A few years ago, the *Los Angeles Times* published an article in which environmental experts tested bacteria levels of 250 beaches in California, and do you know which beach was at the top of the list?"

"Let me guess, Kiddie Beach," I said jokingly not knowing the correct answer.

19

"That's right!" She continued, "As if it wasn't bad enough that we already have bad air quality because of these polluting power plants, Oxnard's 'Kiddie Beach' was named the most polluted beach in Southern California by an 'expert' environmental group! Even our waters are polluted. And how many signs did you see up warning *La Raza* of this health hazard? None! Not even in English, much less Spanish! They don't care about these kids or these parents at the Kiddie Beach 'cuz they know they all Brown!"

"Dang. I guess that is kind of messed up." I agreed. "They should at least tell them and give them a chance to make an informed decision as to whether they jump in this toxin-infested water."

"You guess? Homie, you better know!" She asserted while pointing at me with her index finger. "But wait, there are more things that show that they don't care about us."

"Like what?" I replied as I covered my eyes from the glaring sunrays.

"Well, let's start with the restrooms and showers. You see 'em over there?" She pointed unapologetically. "They recently renovated both at the white beach! Women Silver Strand beach-goers can actually sit down while they pee without feeling all disgusted and nasty. Do you feel comfortable enough sitting on the toilet seats at the Kiddie Beach?"

"Hell nah," I laughed out loud.

"That's what I thought!" she exclaimed in a high-pitched tone. "We see this play out in society in general. The government invests in and takes care of places where white

20

people reside and interact. By the same token, the government de-invests in sites that are heavily populated by communities of color. The formula is simple. Wherever white people go, money and resources follow."

"So are you telling me that if more and more white people were to go to the Kiddie Beach, then it will get new bathrooms?" I asked her to clarify the absurd statement.

"Hmm hmm!" She nodded her head up and down. "They have a lot of privilege and as soon as they raise one concern, then it will be taken care of sooner rather than later. We've seen this happen before. Whenever *La Raza* raises an issue, people see it as a complaint, 'Oh they want and ask for everything.' But whenever white people raise an issue, it is seen as an actual concern and must be addressed." She gasped for air and then continued, "Shoot! They will for sure have signs up the next day after the request warning other white families about the toxins in the water. Knowing the politics around here, I bet these signs will be in English only, too!"

"That's True! Why doesn't *La Raza* just walk over and enjoy the cleaner—" I offered, but Jessi cut me off and finished my sentence with the words, "whiter beach?"

"I was going to say cleaner beach, but yeah, whiter beach," I responded.

"You sound like Oxnard's Board of Education in the '70s when they were being sued by Juan Soria and other families for racially segregating students. The Board of Education members said, 'We aren't segregating students intentionally. Mexicans can move wherever they want to, they have the freedom to do so. Blah Blah Blah.' Like homie, it's not that simple! Rent is expensive and ain't nobody trying to give a qualified and educated Mexicana a good paying job," she insisted angrily.

I stayed silent. Again, I thought about how all this was starting to make sense.

She patted me softly in the back, "Also, in case you forgot there is such a thing called racist landlords in Oxnard who do not give people of color a chance to live on their property even if they can afford to do so. My mom, who we both know is a single mother baller, is looking for and can afford a nice house in Oxnard. Despite having a promising conversation with the landlord over the phone, he decided not to let her rent his home after meeting her in person because my mom took my little brother who 'looks' black to meet him. This is 2017! Discrimination with a smile. I swear," she said in frustration while her voice gradually became louder.

"Yeah, you told me about that. That sucks," I said empathetically as I tried to comfort her. "Not to dismiss anything you just said, but what does this have to do with the beach and *La Raza* walking over to the cleaner beach?" I asked innocently.

"That it is not as simple as just getting all your stuff and walking over to the cleaner, whiter beach!" she exclaimed and raised her voice. "Have you ever played *cumbia* or *Chente* out loud at this cleaner beach? White people stare at you like you are some type of alien or something. Like they have never heard Selena before! That shit is degrading!"

"So true," I laughed in agreement.

22

"But there you have Cody over there, bumping his freaking Country music and people act like it's nothing," she said while smacking her lips. "I don't know about you, but I like listening to some *cumbia* and *bachata* while I enjoy my Arnold Palmer Arizona Iced Tea at the beach. I can't do that in peace while I have these white people staring at me as if something is wrong with me. Like, nah homie, something is wrong with *you!*" she exclaimed as she pointed at the white surfers who had just passed us.

"Chill!" I said, trying to calm her down. "Yeah, that's true tho," I agreed and then asked her, "What are some other ways in which this beach segregation stuff is messed up?"

Jessi squinted her eyes against the glistening sun and asked, "Do you see any lifeguards at the 'Kiddie Beach'?" I detected a hint of disgust in her voice.

I looked over to the Kiddie Beach and then replied, "Nope! Well, I think recently they built a lifeguard hut, but to be honest, I don't know if anyone is actually in there."

"There you go," she said confidently, as if her point was validated. "Recently. That's the key word. Probably after someone almost drowned. I learned in my child development class that a child could drown in less than 2 inches of water! From experience, I know that Kiddie Beach is only 'kiddie' two steps in, then after that it goes pretty deep. The more you walk in, of course. The only thing 'kiddie' is that it does not have any waves. But just because there aren't any waves, doesn't mean somebody can't drown!"

"True! I feel like if they really cared about the people at the Kiddie Beach then they'd have like five lifeguards," I said while I shrugged my shoulders in agreement.

"For reals! They should for sure have more than one lifeguard, since, after all, there are a lot of kids there? They want to call it 'Kiddie' beach, but ain't nobody want to kiddie the kids?" she said cleverly. "You see that over there?" pointing at the hot dog stand near the white beach.

"Yeah. It is super nice to have food nearby when you are swimming. Swimming and running gets you so hungry, huh?" I added.

She laughed, "That's besides the point! That's another way *La Raza* at the 'Kiddie' Beach are discriminated against."

"What? How?" I asked impatiently as my eyes widened.

"Well," Jessi said, "must be nice to have immediate access to food on the beach. People at the white beach do not have to cross the busy street and 4-way stop sign to get their snacks from the corner store. They have it right there on the sand, on their laps, like a luxury hotel."

I laughed knowing that we are talking about a hot dog stand and not some fancy food restaurant.

She continued without hesitation, "Do you think they would allow the *elotero* to sell *elotes* and *raspados* at the 'Kiddie' Beach?" "Hell No!" she replied before I could even respond. "As soon as a few Brown kids are spotted sucking on bright yellow juicy *elotes*, the cops will be called and the *raspados* and *elotes* will be confiscated because it is 'illegal' to sell those in Oxnard. But here you have this white lady selling hot dogs, expensive ass hot dogs at that, on the beach in public in front of everyone! With an official stand and sign! Shake my damn head," she complained.

"For reals! It should be 'illegal' to sell hot dogs at that price!" I laughed at my own joke. "Dang. On a serious note, that's messed up. You know I suck at cooking, but even I know that both hot dogs and *elotes* are boiled in hot water. What's the difference? Why can't *eloteros* sell *elotes* at the beach?" I wondered.

"Because this beach is racist AF," she replied without a smile. "Hot dogs are a staple of white American foods, while *maíz* is a staple of Mexican and Indigenous foods. How dare we privilege *elotes* over hot dogs? This is 'Merica!" she said sarcastically.

I laughed out loud knowing how pissed off she gets when people say "this is 'Merica." "That sounds ridiculous, but not far from being the truth. The U.S. is always trying to force people to assimilate and think that there is only one culture. But for reals tho, all this food talk is making me hungry. Let's hit up TDM!" I suggested, knowing that she would agree.

"Only if you agree to go share the knowledge I just dropped on you with all your little Mexican homies who naively hit up the white beach everyday," she responded as she playfully pushed me away.

"Yeah, I will... Only if you pay for my burrito."

*This story was inspired and modeled after my favorite writing by Michele Serros, "Attention Shoppers."

"Stay Classy Oxnard"

The past few years have witnessed a huge push by the school district to increase students' vocabulary at BrownStock Junior High School in Southside Oxnard. Reading tests scores have been historically low, so school administrators have concluded that more exposure to "fancy" vocabulary words would help elevate the dismal tests scores. Like in most cases, BrownStock teachers are issued their directives, but are given very little training and resources to fulfill them effectively. To say the least, they are left on their own to figure it out. The instructions are simple. As long as they were increasing their students' vocabulary, whatever that means, they were following their orders.

And that was when Ms. Gomez took matters into her own hands. She had recently received her teaching credential and her enthusiasm was off the charts. Additionally, she had also minored in human rights and social justice in college. Her interests in social justice stemmed from her experiences and observations she made growing up in Southside Oxnard. Since she was given an opportunity to teach in her community, Ms. Gomez made it her priority to spread the knowledge about social injustices with her eighth grade middle-schoolers.

"Today's word of the day is *internalized racism*," Ms. Gomez spoke excitedly while she smiled and showed her pearly white teeth. Unlike other days, students didn't mumble "who cares" underneath their breaths like they usually do with more traditional, "hard core" academic words such as esoteric or ubiquitous. Instead, they gave Ms. Gomez their undivided attention.

"Has anyone heard of internalized racism?" Ms. Gomez asked, hoping that some of students have come across this notion.

"I have heard of racism, but never of internal... racism," Juanita replied while stumbling trying to pronounce internalized racism.

27

"Internal-ized racism," Ms. Gomez enunciated slowly to help Juanita pronounce it correctly. "Ok. So what does racism mean, Juanita?" Ms. Gomez asked patiently.

"From what I know, racism is when someone discriminates against someone else because of their different skin color or their culture. I watched a video on YouTube that said people become racist because they feel that their own race and culture is better or something like that, well that's what video said," Juanita responded timidly, unsure if she was correct.

"Thank you, Juanita. That's a really good starting point. Of course racism is more complicated than that, but that's a good explanation," Ms. Gomez said in encouragement. "Ok. So what does internalized racism mean?" Ms. Gomez asked the entire class again.

"Internalized means that you believe in what society says, so in this case it means that you believe in racism, right?" Felipe confidently added.

"Not necessarily," Ms. Gomez quickly responded.

Knowing that she was pressed on time since she had to teach the rest of the curriculum, Ms. Gomez wrote the definition on the white board while she read it aloud, "Internalized racism is when people believe in racist attitudes and beliefs towards members of their own ethnic/racial group, including themselves. For example, a Mexican believes that all Mexicans are lazy, which is why they are on welfare." Ms. Gomez continued aloud, "In my opinion, the best way people learn new vocabulary words is through personal examples of ways the vocabulary word has played out in their lives. So, do people in Oxnard experience internalized racism?"

All thirty students stared at her baffled in silence. After a few quiet seconds, Cesar indecisively raised his hand, "I don't know about anyone else, but I experience internalize racism."

"How so, Cesar?" Ms. Gomez responded empathetically.

"When I was little, my family and I would go to the Centerpoint Mall right there on Saviors and Channel Islands. We would go there for everything! Food, toys, clothes. *Mervyn's* was the go-to spot for school uniforms! The *comida China* was bomb and cheap, too. My parents would feed a family of six for less than 20 dollars, I swear! Aside from going with my family, I would go with friends, and sometimes alone. I went there to buy my skateboarding stuff from the A-Z Toys store. I was there every other day."
Ricardo interrupted impatiently, "I remember that store! I was almost sponsored by them for my skateboarding skills at age 11!"

"That's impressive, Ricardo," Ms. Gomez said impressed of his accomplishment.

"Yeah, me too," Cesar said as he complimented his smile with wink toward Ms. Gomez. He continued, "Anyways, as I got older, I intentionally did not go there anymore. As a matter of fact, I started calling it 'CheddarPoint Mall,' like everyone else did."

"What do you mean by Cheddar?" Ms. Gomez asked Cesar to clarify.

29

"Cheddar, like Mexican, Wetback. You know. It's hella racist," he claimed, "It was an insult to shop there because there were a lot of Cheddars there. I would even make my family drive me 20 minutes all the way to the Ventura mall just to buy shoes because I thought everything sold at Centerpoint Mall had to be fake since there were so many Mexicans."

"That's so true," agreed classmate Angelica. "I stopped shopping there, too, after I was made fun of for being a '*chunti*' and 'Cheddar' for taking pictures with my besties at that mall."

"Yeah, I hate to admit it, but I internalized the racism," Cesar confessed aloud, "They sold Mexican *musica, sombreros,* and *botas vaqueras,* so it made sense to call it CheddarPoint Mall. All that was embarrassing. Little did I realize that I am Mexican and my dad dressed like that, so I should be prideful! Instead, I was basically putting down my own family and culture. What for? I don't even know. I guess it wasn't 'cool' to be Mexican."

"Well, that's how internalized racism works," Ms. Gomez patted him on the back, "People put down their own kind because they have internalized the belief that their own skin color and culture is less than, so it must be corrected or changed. Thank you for sharing your personal experience, Cesar. That's a really good example of how internalized racism happens in Oxnard. We have time for one more example. Does anyone care to share?"

"Do you know what Instagram (IG) is?" Alejandra immediately asked Ms. Gomez.

"Wow! Of course I do! What are you trying to say? Do I look that old?" Ms. Gomez replied sarcastically as her cheeks blushed uncontrollably. The class laughed.

"I think I know of an example of internalized racism that connects to IG."

"What is it?!" Ms. Gomez asked anxiously.

Alejandra continued, "Me and a lot of my friends follow this account called 'StayClassyOxnard' on IG,"

Esmeralda interjected, "Oh my god, that page is so hilarious."

"I thought that page was funny, too, until this conversation happened," Alejandra challenged Esmeralda. "Every other day, this account posts pictures of people from Oxnard, mostly *La Raza,* or at least it is assumed it is, doing 'ghetto' things. So, basically the name 'StayClassyOxnard' is sarcastic because all they do is make fun of people from Oxnard because they are the opposite of 'classy.' It's obvious that many people who are featured in the pictures are trying to do whatever they can with the scraps they are given. For example, recently this account posted a picture of a car that uses a *trapo* as a windshield wiper. Not everyone can afford a new windshield wiper. When you are poor, you have to improvise and make do with what you have."

Julío intervened compassionately, "That's facts! My family does this all the time. My *tío* installed a house stereo in his car when his car stereo burned a fuse. Sure it looked funny and 'ghetto,' but it bumps. That's all that counts for me. It works."

"'StayClassyOxnard' also makes fun of homeless people, too," Erica shouted from the back of the classroom. "My best friend's *primo,* who is homeless, was featured on this account sleeping in a shopping cart. Yeah, it may seem funny at first, but one, he is homeless, and two, he also has a mental illness. Instead of receiving medical help or some shelter, he got 200 likes on IG. Those 'StayClassyOxnard' IG followers are no innocent bystanders!" Some of Erica's classmates stared at her, speechless, knowing that they liked some of those pictures.

Noticing that she had already spent 10 minutes on the word of the day, Ms. Gomez interrupted, "Yes, that's another great example of how people in Oxnard have internalized not only racism, but also classism, as pointed out by Erica. Usually the internalization of isms is subconscious and seen as a joke, but in the long run, it has serious consequences. People end up hating themselves and their communities. Internalized racism also keeps stereotypes alive. Before I went to college and learned about internalized racism and other topics, I hated and was ashamed to be from Oxnard, especially because of its prominent 'cheddar' population. As a matter of fact, I would say that I am from Ventura or Camarillo. But now I challenge people whenever they are putting down their own people, especially my own *gente* from Oxnard. You all should do the same," Ms. Gomez said proudly as she stared deeply into the eyes of her students.

"Anyways, tomorrow we'll talk about gentrification and whether it is happening in Oxnard," Ms. Gomez offered in a suspenseful tone.

"How do you spell that?" Leonardo asked with pen in hand and ready to write it all down.

"Come to class tomorrow and you will find out," Ms. Gomez promised.

Forget Microsoft Word

In recent years, the Chican@ Studies program at the local community college in Oxnard has struggled to fill its courses. On one hand, administrators and some faculty in other disciplines and departments speculate the reason is because it is not a "real" college major and few jobs pay enough after graduation, so there are few incentives to major in it. On the other hand, Chican@ Studies *profes* argue that there is not enough institutional support. In particular, they claim that much of the college's money and recruitment has been funneled into the science, technology, engineering, and mathematics fields, or STEM. To this, they say that this explicitly and implicitly sends a message to its students suggesting Chican@ Studies simply does not matter.

This semester, only four students enrolled in the "Introduction to Chican@ Studies" course—three *Mexicanos* (Luís, Jimmy, and Jorge) and one *Mexicana* (María). *Profe* Perez still offered the course regardless of low enrollment because she is a firm believer in the idea that quality is always better than quantity. The discussion is much better when there are fewer students for two reasons: they are prone to get to know one another and they can't hide in the back of the classroom. In addition, she knew that if the college didn't allow her to teach the course, then she could confirm that the college itself is undeniably unsupportive of Ethnic Studies, and thereafter racist.

Like previous semesters, the first day of class was unforgettable. *Profe* Perez did not mess around. As soon as the four students sat down, she played a documentary about Manifest Destiny, or the belief that the expansion of the United States throughout the North American continent was justified because Indigenous folk and *Mexicanas/os* were "savages" who needed to be "civilized" and "saved."

Before reflecting on the documentary, *Profe* Perez thought it would be a good idea to know each other's names, so she proceeded with a roll call. "María del Refugio Barajas?"

35

"Here," María replied immediately without hesitation.

"Luís Alberto Magaña?" *Profe* Perez looked at the students.

"*Presente Profe*," Luís said fluently in Spanish as he emphasized "*profe*."

"Jaíme Peña?" After five silent seconds, no one raised their hand. "Jaíme?" *Profe* Perez repeated as she scanned the four students in the class. Again, not a single acknowledgement. "Jaíme Roberto Peña?" *Profe* Perez asked impatiently one last time.

"Oh, it is Jimmy, I go by Jimmy, please call me Jimmy," Jimmy said after hearing his middle name called out.

All three students as well as the *Profe* stared at him confused. Instinctively, *Profe* Perez saw this as an opportunity to connect to Manifest Destiny and future discussions.

"So Jimmy, why do you go by Jimmy as opposed to Jaíme?" Profe Perez asked curiously.

"Hmmm . . ." Jimmy pondered aloud while scratching his chin. "Well, a couple reasons. One, no one has ever challenged me on this name. In fact, my high school teachers preferred to call me Jimmy as opposed to Jaíme because it was too difficult to pronounce, which I agree with."

He continued naively, "Second, and I think this is the real reason, I have always gotten As in all my classes. I am a really good student. Specifically, I am really good at following directions. I say all that to say that whenever I write a paper, I always do a spell check on my computer. Those are the directions my teachers give me, so I follow them closely.

Microsoft Word makes a squiggly red line underneath Jaíme, but it doesn't do so underneath Jimmy. So, I automatically assumed that Jimmy is the correct version of my name. And that's why I go by Jimmy."

Profe Perez is well aware that the Americanization of Jaíme's name is precisely a result of Manifest Destiny. By that twisted colonial logic, Jaíme's birth name is "savage-ish and dirty," while Jimmy is "civilized and clean."

Instead of breaking it down for him and for everyone else, *Profe* Perez opened up the floor for discussion by asking, "Does anyone care to respond to Jimmy's explanation about his preferred name?"

Jorge raised his hand confidently, "By the way, my name is Jorge, we didn't get to me yet" he continued as he looked directly at Jimmy. "I see direct connections between Jimmy's explanation and the short documentary we just watched. It seems to me that your name, Jaíme, has been colonized. We live in a hyper white supremacist society, so we are automatically expected to assimilate and forget about our cultural ties. Sometimes this means changing our Indigenous or Mexican sounding names to more "American," English sounding names in hopes that we will be accepted by this society."

"I agree," María interjected unapologetically, "You don't even know how many times my white teachers and so-called white friends have called me 'Mary'? Every single time, I correct them, 'Like no honey, it's María del Refugio, to be exact. C'mon! Sound it out, Ma-rí-a!' I do this because I care

37

about my *cultura*, my peoples, my histories, *mi lengua*, even though I know it's the colonizer's lingo."

Jimmy quietly stared at his laptop and pretended he was taking notes. He had never been asked to think critically about his cultural identity or experience. In fact, he had never taken an Ethnic Studies course, and this conversation now threw him off completely. Knowing that tension was building, *Profe* Perez joined the conversation to center the system at play instead of focusing on Jimmy as an individual. "So from where do we get the messages that our *cultura* is inferior and in need to be civilized and saved?"

Jorge raised his hand, "I think we get it from everywhere! Movies, TV shows, social media, books, teachers, and so on. But I want to acknowledge that Jimmy's example of Microsoft Word encourages us to think of important, yet subtle ways our *cultura* is inferior-ized."

"That's right," María shouted with excitement. "My older cousin, Ramón, just graduated from a four-year university last year. Can you believe that the university did not allow for him to put the accent over the 'o' in his first name for his degree? Making him Raymond! I don't even know where to begin to analyze what messages that sends to him, his parents and siblings, and even his future kids. I'll tell you this for sure, that's one way universities bring down our *cultura.*"

Jimmy's face turned red out of frustration and confusion. Without hesitation, he said in a loud and firm tone, "From now on, don't call me Jimmy anymore, *por favor* CALL ME

JAÍME!" He continued with a mixture of excitement and frustration, "I am beyond ashamed of how I have internalized these negative messages about myself, *mi familia, y mi cultura.*"

Before *Profe* Perez approached him for comfort, Jaíme stood up and yelled, "You know what, forget Microsoft Word!" Out of frustration, he picked up his semi-brand new *manzana* laptop and threw it at the nearest wall. The screen cracked and the space bar flung out of the keyboard.

Everyone, including *Profe* Perez, looked at him in encouragement. "Could it be?" The class wondered collectively. The Chican@ spirit had entered his body right before everyone's eyes.

Luís stood up on his chair and shouted back while raising his Brown fist, "Yeah, forget Microsoft Word!"

Hablando Español sin Vergüenza

Jacobo rarely took the local Scatt bus in Oxnard. Not because he was ashamed or could not afford it. The real reason was because it took too long. Why take 45 minutes to get somewhere, when he could get there on a skateboard in just 15, he complained? To him, the Scatt bus was always tempting just for the sake of the ride and experience. Since poor people and drug addicts rode it the most, he had heard that $1.50 paid for a ride *and* entertainment. One time, he and his friend, Tomas, took the Scatt bus to T-Shirt Warehouse because they were too tired to skate there. Well, Tomas was tired, but Jacobo had just gotten new shoes, so he didn't want to get any blisters.

Anyways, on this ride, Jacobo got his money's worth. Unfortunately, he did not witness a fight nor did he see someone singing and dancing as if they were auditioning for "America's Got Talent" for some spare change. Instead, he learned a valuable lesson that he would never forget. He learned that he himself is the glue of his Oxnard community. This means that he holds his community together and keeps it running. Because he is bilingual, it could be argued that he plays a bigger role than the city mayor.

As a Mexican American growing up in Southern California, he learned and spoke Spanish. In fact, both of his parents spoke only Spanish. Although his entire immediate family communicated in Spanish in and out of their home, he had gradually become ashamed and was unwilling to speak Spanish in public anymore. This was in spite of living in a predominantly Spanish-speaking neighborhood. To be sure, on this timely bus ride, he learned of all the important responsibilities he could fulfill because of his ability to speak two languages.

About ten minutes into their bus ride, an elder Mexican lady pushing an old shopping/laundry cart climbed in the bus, approached Jacobo, and asked him the following question,

"*¿Mijo, qual es la parada para la clinica de salud en la Calle Jota?*"

Jacobo understood her question perfectly since he spoke Spanish, yet still he responded, "In three stops."

The lady squinted her eyes as if she had just tasted something sour and immediately replied, "*¿Que? ¿Que significa eso?*"

Jacobo looked at her, remained silent, and raised three fingers so she could at least understand his hand gesture while he offered slowly, "In three stops, you get out."

Again, she stared at him with confusion.

When her stop approached, Jacobo said, "here" and pointed to the nearest door. The lady replied, "*gracias*," and then exited the bus.

Observing this injustice unravel in front of his eyes, Tomas softly shoved Jacobo, "Why did you do that?"

"Do what?" Jacobo asked.

"Don't you speak Spanish fluently? Why didn't you just respond to that lady in Spanish? That would have avoided her confusion," Tomas explained.

"Yeah, I speak Spanish, but I don't understand why I have to speak it all the time. After all, don't we live in America? The official language of this country is English, so why can't I speak English," Jacobo answered in frustration.

"You're trippin'," Tomas gently pushed him again. "I wish I spoke multiple languages. Especially since I live here in Oxnard. I would speak whatever non-English language unapologetically because I know how much of a difference it makes. 'Til this day, I feel some type of way because my parents never taught me Spanish."

"What do you mean?" Jacobo asked in sincere curiosity.

"Well, if you live in Oxnard and you know how to speak both Spanish and English, then you pretty much have the key to the city. You know how it is here in Oxnard? There are a lot of people who only speak Spanish, so if you speak Spanish, then you would be able to communicate with all of them without skipping a beat. You know this would make it that much easier to purchase Mexican *paletas* at the swap meet on Sundays. Truth be told, you might even get a Spanish-speaking discount," Tomas laughed.

"Nah, but for reals, aside from the conversations at grocery stores or restaurants, if you are bilingual in Oxnard, then you are in a position to make a huge impact on the community. Do you remember my *primo* David?" Tomas asked Jacobo.

"The one that is hella light-skinned with blonde hair and green-ish eyes?" Jacobo responded confidently.

"Yeah. That's him. He speaks Spanish fluently, too, since his parents only speak Spanish. Whenever I visit him, I noticed that he always translates for both of his parents. As a matter of fact, last week during our back-to-school night, he served as the official translator between his mom and his teacher. I am telling you. Every single time, he gets down with interpretations in and out of school settings, and for free, too. The school should pay him for doing that," Tomas asserted while shaking his head.

43

"I have done that, too," Jacobo replied while he tapped his chest twice, complimenting himself.

"Every month I interpret my dad's medical bills for him and I also pay most of the bills. Well, my parents technically pay them, but since I speak English, I am their bill payer representative. I am the one who speaks with the customer service person at the front desk," Jacobo shared.

"You see that is exactly what I am talking about! Imagine if you went on strike and decided not to interpret for your parents? Not only would you get an ass whooping, but your parents would also be so lost without you. Your dad would not be able pay his bills or get his prescriptions. Besides that, y'all would not have cable! No more SpongeBob," Tomas said only half jokingly.

Jacobo smiled, "Well, if I play such an important role in my community because I can speak two languages, then why don't we have more bilingual classes in our schools?"

"I am still trying to figure that out, too. It doesn't make sense to me either," Tomas responded and shrugged his shoulders.

"I wish my *tío*, Roberto, was here to explain it to us. Because he was ashamed to speak Spanish growing up, he wrote a research paper on bilingual education for his senior capstone project at his university. From what I remember, he said that the thought of his native tongue, Spanish, being inferior to English was a notion that was taught to him indirectly early on in his childhood through his schooling," Tomas added.

Jacobo listened quietly and carefully.

Tomas continued, "He talked about how English-only speaking programs and initiatives in the schools he attended solely focused on the advantages of speaking English fluently and intelligently, rather than emphasizing the importance and necessity of being bilingual. This confused him because his parents also relied on him as a translator everywhere they went—from grocery stores to school. Because of this, he has always wondered how and why California, which has one of the largest bilingual-speaking populations in the United States, would not only exterminate bilingual programs, but also discriminate against students who spoke Spanish. It puzzled him that a state with so many bilingual speakers would get rid of a program that would ultimately benefit its students, communities, and perhaps smoothen educational experiences of native Spanish speakers."

"Yeah, it doesn't make sense to me either. Why would they take away something so crucial to our existence as Spanish speakers? I can relate to your *tío*. For sure. That sounds like a cool project. Did he talk about why our schools ended bilingual programs?" Jacobo wondered.

"I know he did, but it was about a year ago, so I can't remember everything. I do remember a couple things that stood out." Tomas confessed. "I remember he included a meme of a Latino dishwasher that read, '*Antes no sabia Ingles y era lavaplatos. Ahora sé Ingles y soy* dishwasher,' to underscore the idea that English equals success. This is one reason. According to my *tío*, people in the U.S. erroneously

45

believe that if you learn English, then you will automatically be more successful, yet the meme argues otherwise. To him, it's not that simple—a big issue is discrimination based around skin color or looks. So even if people learn English perfectly, but they dress or look a certain way, then they will not be hired," Tomas said with frustration.

"Yeah. I have seen this happen before," Jacobo replied. "My neighbor graduated from high school with English honors and community college where he minored in English, but because he has a tattoo on his neck and he's brown, he has not been able to get a stable, decent-paying job."

"By the way, our stop is coming up." Jacobo reminded Tomas.

Tomas nodded his head in agreement. "I also remember my *tío* talk about how languages and cultures in the U.S. are ranked from best to worst. English is seen as the best, so every other language is looked down upon. He gave an example of how Native Americans were stripped from their own unique ways of speaking, knowing, and living because they were different than white Americans. He then connected this to what had happened in 1998, when California officially passed a law to ban bilingual education. He said that people in power were uncomfortable with the idea that they could not understand a conversation because then they can't control it."

Jacobo smacked his lips, "All this is starting to make sense to me. My teachers don't allow me to speak Spanish in class because they probably think I am talking smack about them behind their backs . . . which I probably am. They suck.

I swear. But anyways, in this case, I have more power than they do. That's so dope. I never thought about it like that."

Tomas laughed, "Yeah. I wish I was in your position. You should call my *tío* Roberto. He'll tell you why it is so important for you to continue to serve as a translator and mediator for your community. He talks about it all the time because he says bilingual youth don't understand their important roles in keeping the Oxnard community running."

"I will," Jacobo responded excitedly.

"Rose Ave and Gonzales Rd," announced the loud speaker in the bus.

"Pull the cord, here's our stop!" Jacobo yelled impatiently while rushing toward the door with his skateboard.

47

The Dallas Cowboys are Coming to Town

I will forever have mixed feelings about the National Football League's (NFL) often-acclaimed "America's team," the Dallas Cowboys—especially their world famous navy blue star. For as long as I could remember, the Dallas Cowboys have held their summer training camp practices sporadically in Oxnard. Around late-August of every summer, spectators travel from cities and states hundreds and thousands of miles away, then exit the 101 freeway just to watch the Cowboys practice in my hometown.

As these spectators would exit toward the northwest side of the city, down Vineyard Avenue, they would be greeted with city-sanctioned Dallas Cowboys banners from previous summer camps plastered over almost every single street light along the road to the practice site. Whereas spectators are welcomed with Cowboys pole banners, similar to Christmas banners and holiday decorations in December, nearby local Oxnard residents are constantly reminded that their street parking is extremely limited during the Cowboys training camp. This is mainly because the city wants to make money off spectators by having them pay a "small" fee of $20 for parking. And for us Oxnardians, this all makes it difficult to find street parking for our own homes.

While most people, including myself, would be beyond excited to finally see our hometown talked about in a positive light for once via sports channels such as ESPN, the coverage mostly rehashed our wonderful, ocean-breeze-just-the-right-amount-of-sun-everyday weather. Despite our very little TV fame, having the Cowboys come to Oxnard never seemed right to me because of the context of the city. As I grew older, it became obvious to me that there were far more disadvantages than advantages associated with the Cowboys coming to Oxnard. In the long run, the very little TV fame was not worth it at all.

Given my natural researcher instinct and my curiosity in general, I have low-key (aka informally) surveyed and collected responses by both insiders and outsiders about what comes to mind when they think of Oxnard. By far, the four most common responses are *la playa, fresas,* boxing, and *cholos,* specifically *La Colonia,* a *barrio* and gang in Oxnard. *La Colonia Chiques,* stemming out of the impoverished *La Colonia barrio,* is considered one of Ventura County's largest and deadliest gangs. Because of this, the main narrative revolving around Oxnard is almost always negative and criminal-ridden. Stories about Oxnard are filled with gang violence, drugs, and criminals.

La Colonia Chiques and the Dallas Cowboys share something very important—they both utilize the Cowboy star to express their association and commitment to an organization. While Dallas Cowboys fans wear official team apparel to showcase their loyalty, *La Colonia Chiques* gang members also sport the Cowboy star to showcase their loyalty to their gang. In other words, the "official" logo of *La Colonia Chiques* is the Cowboy star. After all, the removal of the "w" on Cowboys T-shirts and jerseys forms the words "CO BOYS," short for "*Colonia* Boys."

This is precisely why I have mixed feelings about the Dallas Cowboys coming to Oxnard to practice. If we are so concerned with gang-related issues, does the city of Oxnard truly benefit from hosting Cowboys practices? If so, beneficial for whom? How is the money raised through the Cowboys camp actually invested back into the city, especially highly impoverished, run-down areas such as *La Colonia*? Because the benefits that come along with hosting practices haven't been explicit and/or intentional, it always seemed counterintuitive to me to bring a team that would further criminalize the already hyper criminalized, *La Colonia Chiques.*

In my early teens, my sports interests shifted from fútbol to football. Because I was skinny and fast, I naturally played wide receiver and cornerback. Like most children, I idolized and mimicked NFL football players while I played football in the alleys and streets of the Blue Ghetto with my friends. Terrell Owens (T.O.), a then-professional wide receiver for the Dallas Cowboys, was one of my favorite NFL players and he was certainly part of my mimicking repertoire.

I liked T.O. not only because he caught everything thrown his way, but mainly because of his arrogance and charisma, especially after scoring a touchdown. T.O. was known for going overboard when it came to touchdown celebrations. Without his celebrations and dances, football would not be nearly as entertaining. My favorite celebration was when he took popcorn from a fan and threw it through his facemask as if he was eating it. Needless to say, he was tight AF. Despite my infatuation with T.O.'s never dull moments on the field, in the back of my mind, I knew I could not rock his Cowboys jersey anywhere in my city. Despite wanting one desperately, I never asked for or bought a T.O. jersey because I knew it entailed me getting into trouble, moreso with the police than with other gang members.

In Oxnard, CA it is practically forbidden to wear Dallas Cowboys apparel—I read on *Los Angeles Times* that at one point of time it was the only city in the nation where wearing Dallas Cowboys fan gear could draw a fine or six months in jail. At best, a Brown person wearing a Cowboys jersey in Oxnard would probably result in a minor altercation with the police. This isn't surprising. Around 2004, the city of Oxnard successfully sought out a gang injunction program in hopes of reducing gang-related homicides and crimes. The Oxnard injunction established a 10 p.m. curfew and prohibited gang apparel, flashing gang signals, and associating with other identified *La Colonia Chiques* gang members in public.

More than anything, the Oxnard gang injunction program allowed for a highly subjective interpretation on the part of officers when determining who is labeled and thereafter targeted as a gang member. In other words, the criteria used to determine who is gang member provided officers with a tremendous amount of flexibility to label anyone, including youth, as a gang member. This is mainly because it relied heavily on second-hand sources of information, interpretation of body language, dress, hearsay, and incorrectly profiling youth based on geography and residence. Had I bought and worn a T.O. Cowboys jersey, I could and would have probably been mislabeled as a gang member, even though I do not and have never self-identified as a gang member. Unfortunately, this also means that I would be targeted and penalized as a gang member, too.

In 2014, the city of Oxnard did one of the most unsettling, illogical, contradictory things ever. They agreed to have the Dallas Cowboys scrimmage the Oakland Raiders.

While at first glance this may not seem problematic, the problem arises when you take into consideration that *Southside Chiques*, a rival gang of *La Colonia Chiques* also located in Oxnard, wear Raiders. Why would the city of Oxnard agree to this knowing that this would not only encourage Oxnard residents to wear "gang-affiliated" apparel, but would also create even more turmoil amongst local gangs? From a resource development standpoint (i.e. grants), this makes perfect sense. It's strictly business.

An often hidden fact is that the quantity of crime statistics that a city/police department generates determines the amount of money that can be generated from crime reduction grant sources. In other words, the more "crime" a city has, the more money that city will receive to help reduce it. This makes sense since we all want a reduction in crime. However, when looking at it more closely, it becomes obvious that because of the interests of making money for the city, there is an inclination on behalf of the police department to label as many people as possible as *cholos*, even though they might not self-identify as such. Therefore, instead of saying, "It takes money to make money," one can say, "It takes crime to make money." This is known as the prison-industrial complex, which is a term used to describe the overlapping interests of government and industry that use surveillance, policing, and imprisonment as solutions to economic, social, and political problems.

I often hear people from my own town complain, "Don't dress like a *cholo* and you won't be harassed by the police." I

53

have very little patience when I hear this response because I am aware of how a gang injunction operates. I am aware that there is an overwhelming mislabeling of youth and adults as gang members. I am aware that regardless of my degree and pursuit of a doctoral degree, because of the color of my skin and preference of clothing, I can be considered a *cholo* and thereafter harassed as one if I wear my shirt one size too big. Or if I accidently don't wear a belt and let my pants sag. Or if I wear my hat backwards because I know that's the style. Or even if I have a bald fade with a line up just because I like that hairstyle. Or worse, if I am a teenager wearing my favorite player's Cowboys jersey because not only do I want to mimic him by doing dances of my own while playing football, but I also want to rock his jersey while doing so, as I should be able to.

*This story was informed by the report, "A Report on Systemic Mismanagement of Program and Conflict of Interest Practices within the City of Oxnard and its 'Gang Suppression' Operation," prepared by the League of United Latin American Citizens, Ventura County, California.

Are You on Probation?

During a beautiful, ordinary Oxnard summer day, David's girlfriend invited him to a BBQ community party at the intersection of Wooley Road and Victoria Avenue, near the Oxnard Harbor. This is one of the wealthier sides of the city. Initially, he did not want to go because he was aware that the community is made up of predominantly white retirees. He knew that he and his girlfriend would be the only two Mexicans at this BBQ, but they decided to go as soon as they found out it was going to be catered by Wood Ranch BBQ &

Grill—something they could not pass up. Not surprisingly, as soon as he arrived, David immediately noticed that this BBQ was composed of older white folks, some of whom told him they came to Oxnard solely to retire—this scene confirmed his hypothesis that these people weren't originally from Oxnard.

About half an hour into this party, something happened that David had never seen before at any point in his 19-year lifespan in Oxnard. Two police officers came to the BBQ just to hang out, chat, and eat. As a matter of fact, both officers spoke aloud into the microphone to share with everyone the importance of sustaining strong ties between community and law enforcement. After their speeches, they passed out business cards and spoke individually to whomever approached them with concerns or questions. They even gave out signs in favor of supporting the police; locals agreed to put these signs in their front lawns. David was in extreme culture shock. Not because people actually took the signs, but because this is something that never happens, well, at least not to him. Usually whenever he had seen officers at house parties, it had been to relay a complaint and/or shut it down. They rarely show up proactively to hang out and play with the kids. More likely than not, the presence of the police and subsequent interactions have been overwhelmingly negative rather than positive.

'Til this day, David feels some type of way about the police because he has personally seen and experienced law enforcement break families apart. Such rupture among families has not necessarily been through gun violence, such as the shooting and death of a family member, but through other means of policing. While he was an undergraduate at UCLA, he would go home every other weekend to visit family and friends. On one of these visits to Oxnard, his neighbor and childhood best friend, Rogelio, took his mom's car to visit his three-year-old son at his girlfriend's house about a ten-minute drive away. On his way back, Rogelio was pulled over by the police because he had run a red stoplight near his home. Unfortunately, he did not have a driver's license, so the officer decided to give him a ticket and have the car towed. Because this all took place outside of Rogelio's home, his mom urged the older brother and David to reason with the cop to only give him a ticket without having the car towed.

While Rogelio cried for forgiveness and David served as a mediator, Rogelio's older brother pleaded with the police officer by explaining to him how expensive it would be to regain possession of the car after it was towed and how the family was not stable financially. Rogelio's older brother made it clear to the officer that their family was not in a position to pay excessive bills. Despite this respectful and persuasive plea, the officer wasn't having it and had the car towed anyway. This decision on behalf of the officer resulted in a physical fight between Rogelio and his older brother, and resulted in Rogelio being kicked out of their home. Needless to say, having this incident unfold right before his very eyes was beyond traumatizing for David.

The aforementioned incident reminded David that dehumanization plays a vital role in how he and his community are currently policed. In other words, for the officer to proceed with towing the car after being told by Rogelio's older brother that it would both jeopardize family relations and put the family in even more of a financial bind is dehumanizing in and of itself. Having grown up in Oxnard, a city filled with waiting-to-happen police altercations, it is difficult for David to envision effective and successful policing strategies.

As early as his pre-teens, he was greeted by police officers with "Are you on probation?" or "What are you up to?" These are some taken-for-granted phrases that his friends and him have become accustomed to when interacting with the police. Because of this, he wondered, how can there possibly be an effective conversation following those greetings if he is automatically assumed to be up to no good? To this, he also wondered how he can begin to have respect for the law and law enforcement, if he himself is so persistently disrespected from the get-go? Even though David has never been on probation, he would question himself as to whether he should be because these phrases have been directed towards him frequently.

After hearing something over and over again about oneself, one begins to internalize it. This is extremely dangerous, especially in a city with a negative reputation like Oxnard. If negativity is all that is talked about, it is more likely that people will internalize those portrayals and amount to something negative. While this is not always the case, it certainly happens. Psychologists call this self-fulfilling prophecy, which is a term used to describe when a person unknowingly causes a prediction to come true because he/she/they and everyone around that individual expects it to come true. For example, if a parent constantly tells or insinuates that someone is a *cholo* and treat that person accordingly, then sooner than later that individual will internalize that image and begin to act like one. To some extent, this is precisely what happens in Oxnard. Policing tactics that David has been a victim of—such as being presumed to be on probation—have taken a major toll on him physically and emotionally. His soul has been damaged and these negative experiences have led him to be skeptical of law enforcement, especially in his own hometown.

In the midst of community-police tensions across the nation, a phrase that immediately comes to David's mind is community-oriented policing. He has heard this phrase thrown around and talked about as the most effective form of policing not only across the country, but also in Oxnard. In summer 2016, the *Ventura County Star*, a local newspaper, published an article stating that the growing crime rate in Oxnard has encouraged the Oxnard Police Department to return to a community-oriented strategy, which is said to have historically helped reduce the problem. But what exactly does this mean? Who defines what community is? Whose streets are the streets of Oxnard? To put it simply, community-oriented policing has been defined as police officers building ties and working closely with members of the communities in order to better serve their needs and concerns. To David, moreover, it means something more than that.

David imagines community-oriented policing equating to a relationship filled with true love and care. To him, community-oriented policing means that police officers live in the communities they police. It means that their children go to school with the children they police. It means that both police officers and community members know each other on a first-name basis and not because of negative altercations, but because of genuinely positive ones. It means that although police officers do not necessarily have to look like the people they police, they absolutely have to understand them. Not only in a traditional sense when thinking about different languages, but also in the sense of thinking about sub-cultures. For example, police officers must understand that sagging pants do not equate to being a "thug" or *cholo*. Rather, they need to see it as a clothing preference. It means that police officers take time out of their schedule to play with local kids while in uniform to help strengthen bonds.

More importantly, it means that the first words in a conversation among officers and those they police is not "Are you on probation?" Instead, it is more appropriate to approach someone and ask, "I heard your mother lost her job, how's the family doing? Is there anything I can do to help?" However, without a concerted effort to revamp training and a genuine promotion of positive police and community relations, this vision will remain solely in David's imagination.

Plomero Ayuda, "The pipeline is leaking"

My older brother is a *plomero*. He's been in the game for a minute—long enough to successfully establish and sustain his own plumbing company. In the beginning stages of his startup company, he would ask me to help and I would give him a hand whenever I was in town. One day, during our ride-along to our next job, we stopped by Ferguson, the pluming store, to get a water heater. There, my brother ran into a good friend he grew up with. After chatting for about 15 minutes, we went back to the van to make our next job on time. Before turning the ignition, my brother said something to me that I will never forget. Aside from telling me that he has been doing this plumbing thing for a long time and that he's finally getting recognition, he said, "Can you believe it, *carnal*? A lot of my friends from high school are also *plomeros,* but none of them own their own business."

Immediately I thought to myself that this should not be surprising. Still, even though I already knew the answer, I wondered, why is this the case? Since Oxnard schools do not invest in their students' schooling, it is not a coincidence. Similar to how many of my high school classmates are now barbers, it is expected that most of my brother's high school friends are *plomeros*. As a matter of fact, in Oxnard, it is an *exception* rather than an expectation to go straight into a four-year university right after high school. To this day, I have heard two common explanations as to why many of us do not go to a four-year university. First, Oxnard students are not intelligent enough for a university. Second, since Oxnard students do not care about their education, they are less motivated to go to a university because they do not find it important. I disagree with both because I have observed otherwise.

In 2012, the Oxnard Union High School District (OUHSD) held a dedication and ribbon-cutting ceremony for its new Transportation Technology Center at Channel Islands High School. The OUHSD invested thousands, if not millions, on a state-of-the-art facility dedicated to providing students opportunities to familiarize themselves with vehicle maintenance, service, and repair, collision repair and refinishing, and aviation and aerospace transportation services. To put it simply, these fancy words mean that the OUHSD invested lots of money to rear students into becoming car mechanics. Even though school officials claim there are other opportunities aside from working under the hood of a car such as being a mechanical engineer, I am skeptical in believing those opportunities are realistic. I say this because I know way too many mechanics or hard-labor working people and, in contrast, very few mechanical engineers.

The investment in rearing Oxnard students toward being car mechanics begins to explain why very few people from Oxnard go straight to a four-year university for academics. Without a doubt, investing in a car garage sends a direct and indirect message to its students that they will not amount to anything that involves using their "head." On the contrary, a car garage prepares students for manual labor, that is, working with their hands and back, like it always seems to be the case. What would have happened had the district invested in a cutting-edge science laboratory or a sophisticated aerospace facility? How would this influence not only self-perceptions of ability, but also various career endeavors? In my opinion, gestures such as building a new science laboratory make implicit and explicit differences in the self-worth of students. It sends a message to students that they, too, can be scientists one day. This message is very important because we have not been accustomed to seeing people like ourselves as surgeons or scientists.

Like my older brother, I am a *plomero,* too. However, I am not your ordinary *plomero.* Even though we both enjoy identifying and repairing leaks in pipelines, the settings where I do my *plomeria* are drastically different than where my brother does his. For instance, as a *plomero*, I will never spend an entire day under a house literary replacing old pipes with new ones. Instead, I will spend countless hours in a classroom or studying graduation and college enrollment trends. To be clear, in the past decade, educators have used the "educational pipeline" metaphor to explain educational outcomes of students from different backgrounds. The actual pipe is the schools, including all its staff and teachers, while the water supply are the students. The flow of the water is the promotion from grade to grade. Using this pipeline metaphor, one could illustrate how the low numbers of graduates in high school could be seen as a "leak" in the educational pipeline. Thus, the pipeline must be repaired or replaced to do away with the leaking.

Through conversations, ride-alongs, and experiences with my brother who is an actual *plomero*, I have familiarized myself with the science and logic behind *plomeria*. For instance, I have noticed a major and important difference in diagnosis between actual pipes underneath a house and the educational pipeline. When diagnosing an issue in plumbing, the water itself is very rarely the problem. Water is there and will always be there, so *plomeros/as* have to work with it. This often involves swapping angle stops to control the pressure of the water or replacing copper pipes with PEX pipe, which does not corrode over time like copper despite being exposed to acidic water. Regardless, modifications are made and the water remains as is, for the most part. Conversely, when diagnosing the educational pipeline, the water supply (i.e., students) is often the first to be blamed. Common phrases such as "these kids just don't care about their education," "these kids are not as smart as those other ones," or "these kids do not want to learn nor speak English" serve as examples in blaming the water supply. This drastically different approach in diagnosing pipes can serve as a serious focus point for educational conversations to come.

Until we accept the fact that humans have created and continue to manipulate the existing educational pipeline to benefit a particular set of students—middle- to upper-class white—while disadvantaging others who are poor Brown and Black, then the same predicament we are in now will only persist. In Oxnard, the story will remain the same. Students will be led discreetly to occupations that require them to use their "backs" instead of their "heads," so to speak. Just as alarming, these same students will internalize the belief that perhaps labor-intensive occupations were meant for them since they did not do well in school and academics.

This goes without saying; there is nothing wrong with being a *plomero/a,* a mechanic, or even a barber. That is not my point. Their work is necessary. I admire the use of

65

knowledge and hard work spent by *plomeros/as* like my older brother. Likewise, I am aware that this can be a lucrative occupation because I have single-handedly witnessed the incredible financial rewards that come with being a *plomero/a*. Rather, my point is to ask why has it been *my* people working three times as hard to get paid the same as someone who does not work as hard. Similarly, why is it that *my* people are working with their bodies, consequently being exposed to harsher working conditions and thereafter endangering their lifespan? While most will continue to blame the water supply for the leaks in the educational pipeline, I think of alternative explanations. Like a well-informed *plomero/a*, I think and work with reasons that point to the infrastructure—that is, the rusted, old-fashioned pipes.

Rainy Day Schedule

As an icebreaker during the first week of classes in graduate school, my professor asked us to speak about what we did for fun on our time off from school during snow days. Coming from Southern California, I couldn't necessarily relate to this prompt. It hardly rained in Southern California, much less snowed. In fact, where I grew up, it *never* snowed. Despite not being able to relate to this activity, this question triggered something that I remembered doing in junior high school. For the most part, I treated rainy days as snow days.

Rainy Day Schedule

Whenever it rained, I did not go to school. Luckily, given the geographical location I lived in, I did not miss many days of school.

Until recently, I could not stand the rain and I hated getting my clothes and shoes wet. However, in hindsight, it wasn't just the rain itself that discouraged me from attending school. It was moreso the rainy day schedule. Whenever it rained, it seemed as if my entire school schedule changed for the worst. Students weren't given their recess due to weather conditions, so it was bound to be disastrous. Preteens were expected to act like adults. All students were expected to act calm and controlled in spaces that were overcrowded and stuffy. Should we genuinely think that a group of preteens are controllable in a constrained and enclosed environment?

To make matters worse, school staff tended to hyper-police students during these days. If you stepped out of line, literally and not figuratively, you got in trouble. If you spoke in the hallway, you got in trouble. Every little action or gesture that would seem to come naturally to a preteen such as wanting to converse with friends about the newest trends resulted in getting in trouble.

I remember one lunch period during a rainy day schedule, my class could neither play outside nor overstay our time in the cafeteria, so we were assigned to a portable classroom. In this classroom there was a fire extinguisher. Bright, red, and ready to be used. With nothing else to do and an abundance of curiosity, a group of students, myself included, began to mess with it. Unlike me, other students in my class were familiar with how to use one. They knew that in order to actually use it, the safety pin had to be pulled out. I don't recall who did it, but the fire extinguisher went off towards the end of class. White foam-like chemicals went everywhere. In regards to the school's code of conduct, this was an automatic sentence for suspension, a phone call to parents, or at least a trip to the principal's office for the rest of the day. But since it went off at the end of the class period, most of the students involved scrambled. Therefore, I will always remember this as the day I got away from a suspension.

A mixture of hyper-policing and overcrowding of preteen students with very little to do is a recipe for suspension. Because of this, the school-to-prison pipeline comes to mind whenever I think of a rainy day schedule. By the school-to-prison pipeline, I mean high rates of suspensions cause students to miss school and thus remain home; in some cases, given the presence of systemic poverty, students are sent straight into trouble, harm, drugs, or gangs, which then results in them having a higher probability of being arrested. For these reasons, a rainy day schedule haunts me. On rainy days, I stayed home, *inside*, dry and relieved from the school-to-prison pipeline.

Wasting Talent

Why do schools care about your son's braids more than
they care for his grades? —Nas

It seems like every other day, a published study illustrates that Latinas/os/x students are doing horrible academically. In fact, some scholars call it "falling through the cracks" of the educational pipeline. Such educational results no longer surprise me, especially when we take into consideration that Latinas/os/x are severely affected by segregation and consequently bad schools. As for segregation itself, research will tell you that many times it results in multiple forms of oppressive isolation termed double or even triple segregation, where schools Latinas/os/x students attend are not only segregated by race, but they also have a high concentration of poverty *and* face linguistic segregation. In addition, these segregated schools face countless injustices including, but not limited to, the following: less experienced and less qualified teachers; high levels of teacher turnover; less successful peer groups; inadequate facilities and learning materials; less funds allocated per pupil/student; and higher expulsion rates.

Unsurprisingly, the U.S. Dept. of Education Civil Rights Data Collection indicated that my siblings and I attended public high schools (HS) where Latinas/os/x/Hispanic students comprised no less than 72% and reached up to 86% of the overall student body. Further, more than half the students in our school district (59% to be exact) qualify for and/or receive free and reduce lunch. UCLA Historian and Oxnard-native Dr. David García and his colleagues found that these hyper-segregated schools my siblings and I attended are remnants of a long history of mundane racism in Oxnard, California, traced back to the early 1900s, if not earlier, when only "some of the brightest and best of the Mexican children [could be placed] in white classes."

Because of these reasons and more, whenever I hear or think about students "falling through the cracks," I am quickly reminded of my third-oldest brother, "Joe." He was originally named *Job*; however, throughout his childhood, especially in a school setting and during roll call, he was constantly questioned as to why his parents named him "Job," as in a noun to indicate work, with disregard to the well-thought-out meaning behind his name that clearly had a Spanish origin. Thus, he anglicized his name to "Joe" in hopes of avoiding future judgment, mispronunciations, and humiliation, as many people with "non-American" sounding names often do. Job, like a majority of his classmates, was Mexican American; yet, unlike most of his classmates, he was darker-skinned and although he spoke fluent Spanish and did not identify as Afro-Latino, he was frequently mistaken as Black.

Job was beyond ambitious and talented. At around age 15, he had managed to save up enough money to buy a 1992 Honda Civic in the mid-2000s. His self-proclaimed prized car became a platform to showcase his skills, talents, and unique creativity. He "hooked-up" his Civic by personally installing multiple TVs (about ten), neon lights, a stereo, speakers, and redesigning the interior—essentially initiating trends among other car enthusiasts. In fact, he became known in and around the neighborhood for customizing cars, especially installing TVs on car headrests, which later became his bread and butter. Even more astonishing, given that this all preceded today's Internet and smartphones, he learned how to do everything on his own through trial and error. In other words, he tried out various methods and then chose which one worked best, which can be attributed to a lot of effort, practice, and dedication. For instance, before he began working on cars, he experimented with other electronics such as my electric moped/scooter, which he modified by installing a horn, an alarm, and neon lights.

Having so much familiarity with and passion for electronics and car interiors, without a doubt Job could have been a top-notch electrical engineer or perhaps an interior car designer at a reputable automotive company. Truth be told, had he been given the opportunity, we would already have flying cars. In a perfect world, school should have been the place where he honed additional skills and built on his strengths and intellectual abilities. In reality, all he needed was a little bit more education in order to have the credentials that would support his work and more importantly get him that much closer to starting his career.

Instead of receiving what education researcher Angela Valenzuela refers to "authentic caring" at his school, where all the energy is put toward students' needs and teaching is based on genuine relations, Job was singled out and punished by the school staff and teachers. "Offenses" included wearing a pair of Converse (Chuck Taylors) shoes or sagging his pants, which were both perceived as misconduct and gang-affiliated—a prime example that speaks to a drastic disconnect between students' subcultures and school personnel's already established expectations in school.

Furthermore, his double-zero bald fade with a blonde *copete* hairdo gave rise to complications because at the time it was also thought of as gang-related, even though he never self-identified as a gang member. He was criminalized simply

73

because his hairdo, which served as a marker for teachers and other school staff to harass him since it had a negative connotation attached to it. Although I knew that he was talented and creative enough to succeed in the realm of electronics, restrictions such as not being allowed to style his hair in a particular way or express himself via fashion at his school only begin to illuminate some of the complications he encountered throughout his schooling. Why would Job want to continue going to school if his mere preference of clothing results in an educational impediment?

Job, like many Latinas/os/x and Students of Color with potential to succeed, did not finish high school. Despite his charisma, enthusiasm, intelligence, and great sense of humor, he was never given the opportunity to display his strengths and assets in a classroom. His example not only speaks to the under-education of Latinas/os/x, but also the *miseducation* of Latinas/os/x and other Students of Color. Schools, including staff, teachers, and principals, missed out on opportunities to help students like him advance and better themselves simply because youth failed to adhere to minute, non-academic restrictions such as wearing a particular brand or not tucking in a shirt.

Because I personally witnessed the aforementioned story play out as it did, I will never refer to Job as a high school dropout; it is evident to me that he was *pushed out* of school. Being constantly harassed by teachers, school staff, and principals via dress code policies because of what he wore or how he styled his hair all help explain why he and other

Latinas/os/x continue to "fall through the cracks" of the educational pipeline. Further, without the use of this counterstory, my older brother's circumstance and educational outcome could easily be mistaken as him not valuing education or lacking motivation to succeed academically. Even though such majoritarian stories and assertions are made all the time, they are often false and misleading.

I share the story of my older brother Job because I grew up paying close attention to his 2 Pac-inspired analyses of his experiences in and out of school settings. He was the second, but certainly not the last, in my family to be *pushed out* of the educational pipeline. It should be stated that his circumstance was and is not out of the ordinary. In total, *five* of my *six* siblings did not graduate high school. Such results are difficult to grapple with and extremely difficult to explain when taking into consideration my parents' persistence in encouraging us to stay in school and do well. As Parents of Color often do, my parents made sure we understood the importance of an education through their high aspirations for our educational success.

Despite my parents' constant emphasis on education, only my two eldest brothers, who in my eyes were successful academically (i.e., graduated high school) and like Job had a lot of potential, managed to navigate the educational pipeline through high school—and they barely did so. This speaks to powerful structural impediments such as segregation, culturally irrelevant curriculum, inequitable funding and resources, zero tolerance and hyper-surveillance policies, inexperienced teachers, insufficient advanced placement (AP) classes, lack of educational/college information, and so on, which ultimately trumped and overpowered my parents' strenuous efforts to provide an education for their children.

If only my brother Job's school had believed in him, provided him with mentorship and concrete pathways, and taken the time to learn more about his interests in electronics and car interiors, then maybe he could have been as successful as I always imagined him to be. Instead, his teachers referred him to the principal's office because of his clothes, hairdo, and/or behavior, which ultimately resulted in him being *pushed out* of high school. Because our society rewards those with credentials such as high school diplomas and college degrees, students like my older brother Job, who in reality are never even given an opportunity to pursue a college degree, face limited choices and career paths. Without a high school diploma in hand and very little employment available to him, Job was funneled into trouble, shot at, and constantly harassed by the police. Despite not finishing high school, I look up to my older brother, Job, along with all my other siblings, because I know he was and is capable of doing anything in life, but his assets, abilities, and intelligence were unacknowledged by an educational system that never intended for him to thrive.

El Tesoro

I am the youngest of seven, otherwise known as the "baby" of the family or as my mom would say, *tesoro*. Since I was the youngest in the family, I usually got whatever I asked for—calling me spoiled would have been an understatement. While I enjoyed getting mostly everything I wanted materially, given my family's financial constraints, I did not appreciate what it meant to be the youngest of my family until I got older and noticed that my life trajectory was drastically different from my six siblings. I went to college, but they did not. Likewise, it was not until I got older that I realized how much of a privilege it was to be the youngest child in a large family; as the *tesoro,* I was able to observe and learn from my older siblings' actions. I quickly learned the dos and don'ts by vigilantly observing the ways in which my older siblings navigated certain situations.

I learned most from my older siblings' educational decisions. Rather, the educational decisions that were made for them by schools that ill-prepared them. For example, on one hand, I learned from my second eldest brother that simply completing high school does not put one in a better position to continue on with higher education. On the other hand, from my other five older siblings, all of whom did not graduate from high school, I learned that school staff, zero-tolerance policies, and other well-intended initiatives, or lack thereof, could prevent even the smartest, brightest students from graduating and continuing on with higher education. Because of what I witnessed my siblings go through, it became obvious to me that the current educational system as a feature of overall society does not favor People of Color as well as it could and should.

How did I "dodge a bullet" and end up in graduate school? I purposefully use the phrase "dodge a bullet" because it encapsulates the notion that I avoided serious problems, which in the neighborhood I was living in could possibly be as bad as going to jail, joining a gang, or literally getting hit with a bullet. I ask myself that question every so often. I think about the similarities, but also the differences in opportunities between my siblings and me. Similar to my older siblings, I attended a public high school in Oxnard; however, I did not attend the same public school as them.

In my opinion, the public high school I attended was as insufficient as theirs in terms of informing and preparing the entire student population for college. This is an observation I made in hindsight; of course, while I was a student I thought it was better than my older siblings'. Like my older siblings' high school and many public institutions across the nation, my school invested a lot of time and effort in a particular group of "gifted" students (mostly White and Asian) and ensured that they were college-bound. In turn, this practice left the other students (mostly Students of Color) shortchanged—almost as if they had attended an entirely different school with far fewer resources.

Contrary to what my mom believes about my behavior in school, I was not the best student, but I definitely wasn't the worst. I remember having a few clothing articles confiscated due to them being deemed inappropriate, serving detention a handful of times, and even getting a Saturday school. Despite these mishaps, I had one thing in my favor. I was selected to be in a college preparation program for underrepresented, first-generation college students. I intentionally omit the name of the program because it is irrelevant to the overall point I am trying to make. That is, schools need to serve and cater to the entire student population and not just those who are considered "gifted." Likewise, why would I give credit to or praise a program that did something schools should be doing from the get-go? Although this program or variations of it was implemented nationally, there was only one high school in Oxnard that had it, and I happened to attend that school. None of my older siblings had access to a similar program at their schools or even knew such programs existed.

All of a sudden I began to reap the same benefits as the "gifted" group of students even though I was never classified as "gifted." But I was able to accrue such advantages because of my first-generation college student status. Even though I do not attribute how far I have come in terms of education entirely to this program, it was definitely a difference-maker. This program not only taught me practically everything I needed to know about college, including what it takes to get into college and how to apply for financial aid, but it also provided me with resources such as test vouchers and college-application waivers. In particular, this program instilled in me the idea that college was not only feasible, but it was attainable through guidance and resources, which was important since all of my siblings were excluded from college and I did not know anything about higher education, much less about how to get there.

In addition to providing college-related information and resources, this program did something else that I took for granted every day I was in it. This program gave me the opportunity to believe in myself; I was constantly reminded that I was more than capable of succeeding academically, graduating from whatever university I desired, and obtaining a career I would enjoy. Whether it was making a poster of my "dream" school, taking me on fieldtrips to visit universities, exposing me to various college majors and career paths, or giving me advice as to what classes to take in order to put me in a better position to be admitted into a university, these gave me a sense of belonging and worthiness.

In his research article "Note to Educators: Hope Required When Growing Roses in Concrete," Jeff Duncan-Andrade speaks to the importance of educators instilling "critical" hope into our youth, which rejects hopelessness and the false hopes of "cheap American optimism." Moreover, Duncan-Andrade argues that Students of Color from disadvantaged schools and communities should be encouraged and motivated to pursue their endeavors while simultaneously being critically aware of structural impediments (such as inadequate college-going resources and information) and racism, sexism, and classism. Unfortunately, the schools my siblings and I attended catered to and believed in only a particular group of students, without paying any mind to the other students deemed non-college going, but who arguably needed it most. Thus, very little hope, let alone "critical" hope, was instilled in most students.

As a first-generation, low-income student, my academic success in college and pursuit of doctoral studies is raising my family's expectations. Because of my pursuit of a doctoral degree, I am occasionally introduced at family parties and functions as the "smart" one. The one who made it out. However, 'til this day, I will be the first to admit that I was never the "smartest" nor was I ever the "hardest worker" in my family. Still, because of the exclusivity of college-going information and resources, I was given educational opportunities and experiences not afforded to my siblings or many people from Oxnard. To my family, completing high school is a major accomplishment. But I want to do more for them, for me, and for my community. As the *tesoro*, I have witnessed too many people from my community, including my own family, be excluded from an education—their experiences fuel my interests to pursue a graduate degree and to examine the various factors that simultaneously prevented the educational access of my siblings yet facilitated my own.

rhythm). "Duce! Duce!" became a thing I would say every day. "Duce! Duce!" in a DMX-type voice, just like my coach. Since his voice was deep and mine was definitely not, I had to exaggerate. I did this carefully and hoped I never got caught doing so. He was an ex-NFL running back, and I'm talking a traditional running back, not some half-slot receiver half-halfback, but a 6'2", 260sum-pounds running back. He was a walking muscle, as bulky as they get. Just his presence alone intimidated me and I didn't want to get on his bad side.

The running back on my team was number 22. This is why my coach would say, "Duce! Duce!" For a long time the number 22 held a special place in my heart. As with most organized sports I played, I created some memories I can reimagine over and over again in my head, especially at times when I am down and homesick. However, lately, the number 22 conveys an entirely different meaning in my life.

The Future Leaders of America recently published a study urging for more culturally proficient counselors. In particular, this study illustrated that only 22% of Latina/o/x students who graduate from the high school district I attended in Oxnard are eligible to attend a four-year university. For context, the U.S. Dept. of Education Civil Rights Data Collection found that Latina/o/x students make up 74% of the entire Oxnard high school district student population. This reality is more unsettling than surprising. This simply means that out of 100 Latina/o/x students, only 22 can go to a four-year university in California. It doesn't necessarily mean that they are going to attend a university, but that they have fulfilled the requirements to continue on with their education. In other words, even if a Latina/o/x student in my district worked very tirelessly every single day—as most Americans claim will lead to success and perhaps the "American Dream"—earned a 4.0 grade point average, and graduated from high school, they would not be eligible to pursue a four-year university degree. That's wrong!

I am frequently part of conversations where people struggle with thinking about the limitations of speaking solely about individual agency (aka individual determination) without taking into account structural barriers and impediments (aka lack of college-going resources). Truth be told, I have gotten used to and tired of hearing the phrase, "*échale ganas y todo se puede.*" The fact that a Latina/o/x student from my district can be the perfect student, that is, *le echaron ganas,* and is perfect everything academically, but does not have access to the prerequisites needed to at least be eligible for a four-year university speaks directly to the prevalence of structural barriers.

I once presented these findings along with additional injustices to a class full of hundreds of students. In the audience, a young Black girl raised her hand and innocently asked the following question, "So what happens to the 78% of students who are not eligible to go to a four-year university?" Although I had plenty of responses in mind, I intentionally remained silent without answering her question to make others aware of such a basic, yet vital question. For these

85

"How Come You Didn't Tell Me I Could Do That?"

During the second to last week of classes before Saviers High School graduation in Oxnard, Mr. Blanch made a costly mistake in his classroom. He required all 25 seniors in his government class to give presentations about their future career plans. This would have been a good idea had the school done more for its students to show for. But since most of the students were excluded from college-going resources and information, many were unaware of what exactly they were going to do after high school. In fact, many students in his class were children of Mexican immigrants and the first in their families to graduate from high school, so they were unfamiliar with how the U.S. educational system worked.

Because of this, the presentations were unsurprising, yet unsettling. Almost all students had high aspirations for future endeavors such as wanting to be bankers, lawyers, or doctors, yet very few had an actual plan to put themselves in a better position to achieve these goals. To be exact, out of all 25 students in his class, only one student applied and got into a four-year university. This alarming truth became obvious after only the second presentation.

José went first. His presentation was short, but not so sweet. "I sort of, kind of, have two plans," he offered hesitantly with both his hands in his pocket as he stood shyly in front of the class. "My first plan is to work at the local bank, right here around the corner off 5th street until other opportunities open up for me. My older *primo* told me I could potentially move up and strive for a position as a bank supervisor or a branch manager—that's something he did and he's not so smart, so I can do it, too." José laughed while his classmates stared at him silently, not swayed by his humor.

"Ok." Mr. Blanch intervened, "What's your second plan?"

"My second plan is simple, yet more dangerous." Again, he laughed inconsiderately. "I want to join the military, which I didn't want to do initially. But my friend told me it comes with plenty of benefits, so hey, I am always willing to try new things." A majority of his classmates nodded in agreement as they were in the same boat. They, too, wanted to join the military for similar reasons.

Jazmin, who also considered joining the military, raised her hand and added, "not only does the military come with benefits, but I also heard it looks good on your résumé. Well, at least this is what I was told by Mr. Sanchez, our high school military recruiter. I believe everything he says 'cause after all he could sell water to a well with all his fancy gadgets and Humvee."

The silence was accompanied by you-have-a-good-point head nods in agreement.

"Yeah, so . . . that's it for me, right, Mr. Blanch?" José excused himself and walked to his seat.

"Yes, thank you for sharing. Wish you the best," Mr. Blanch replied. "Enrique you're next."

This is when everything broke loose. Unlike his classmates, Enrique was in an entirely different life trajectory—he was four-year university bound. From the get-go, he began his presentation by listing aloud all nine universities he had applied to.

"Well, I applied to a total of nine schools. Two out-of-state schools, three Universities of California, and four Cal State Universities. But, unfortunately, I only got into six of the nine schools I applied to," Enrique stated casually.

He continued, "The good news is that I have been offered multiple generous financial aid packages from all six universities for my undergraduate studies. In fact, I was pretty much offered a fully funded academic scholarship to Cal State Northridge, which I am seriously considering. After all, who doesn't want a free education?"

"As for my major . . . ," Enrique continued. But before Enrique could talk about his major and career path, Mayra cut him off with a "Whatchu talkin bout Willis" frown on her face, "Hold up! A university!? Without going to community college!? How come you didn't tell me I could do that?"

Enrique stayed awkwardly quiet and looked to Mr. Blanch for help. Enrique did not respond because he was not sure it was his responsibility to explain to everyone the rules to the game for getting to college. He barely knew Mayra—certainly not enough to talk with her about college and career plans. Still, the room remained silent for an extra-long five seconds. Everyone in the classroom but Enrique was wondering the same thing. The daunting silence in the room insinuated that no one had heard of such a thing. To graduate from high school and then go straight into a four-year university is so out of the ordinary. It was certainly unheard of and very rare, especially in Oxnard.

Even Mr. Blanch was in shock. He could not believe that one of his students was admitted to multiple universities. Not being able to take the uncomfortable silence, Mr. Blanch made his second mistake of the day by asking the following question, "By a raise of hands, who in this class applied to a four-year university?"

After three silent, motionless seconds, Enrique raised his hand slowly and cautiously knowing that he was the only one who had applied. The body signals in the crowd were telling—everybody had their arms crossed and wore pouty facial expressions—and the students were infuriated. Again, Mr. Blanch erroneously proceeded by asking, "How come y'all did not apply?"

Immediately, Mayra interjected angrily. She looked directly into Mr. Blanch's gleaming blue eyes, "Because no one told us! Not our teachers. Not our 350-to-1 student counselors. Not our career center person. Not our principal. Not our mamas, but I don't count mine because she does not have an education in the U.S. And not you!" In a sarcastic, yet serious manner, Mayra threw shade at Mr. Blanch and his faced turned red like a *fresa*—almost as if he had just been caught red-handed lying to his own daughter.

The awkward silence remained until Ricardo asked Enrique, "Who told you?"

"Well, my mom's coworker told her about a college-going program for Latino students at a local university, so I applied and I got it. It was really competitive though. Someone told me that three hundred students applied and only sixty got in," Enrique responded depressingly.

He continued, "Had it not been for this program outside of high school, I would have been lost. I swear. In the college-going program I learned that there's a formula to get to college. Just as important, I was also given the ingredients of this formula to get to college. But, I noticed that here at this high school, not only do we rarely talk about the formula to get to college, but as a school in general, we barely even have the ingredients to get there."

"What do you mean when you say formula and ingredients?" Ricardo speculated aloud while the class as a whole also wondered the same thing.

"By formula, I simply mean the university requirements. For example, universities require for you to take the SAT," Enrique replied eloquently.

"The Isssa Who??" Laura joked out loud since she had never heard of that acronym before.

"I forget what it stands for, but it is basically a test you need to take before you apply for college. It supposedly gives the universities a sense of how 'smart' you are and well you will do in college," Enrique said while making air quotes after saying "smart."

"In California, the 'A-G' requirements are important, too. These are the classes you need to take to qualify and be 'prepared' for Cal State Universities and Universities of California. You know, 4-years of English, 3-years of Math, and so on," Enrique recounted.

His classmates had not known these details. In fact, they stared at him in confusion as if he was speaking an entirely different language.

He continued, "Anyways, that's just a couple of the many requirements needed to get into a university. What I mean by ingredients is that some schools make it easier for you to fulfill those requirements. A great case in point are

Advance Placement courses. The more AP classes your school has, the better. Well, that's if you get a chance to enroll in them. Your GPA gets a boost if you take AP classes and if you pass the AP exam, then you automatically get college credits. This is how people save time and/or choose multiple majors." Enrique paused cautiously as he observed that the entire class was silent in both disbelief and anger.

"But it's all the same people in those AP classes. In my entire four years, I never took an AP class nor was I ever encouraged to take one," Joanna complained loudly.

"Exactly, I think we only have eight AP courses total. And it's true, they all go to the same students. I am one of them. But I know of some schools that have over 20 AP courses, so a lot of students can take them. That's why I said that our school rarely talks about the formula and barely has the ingredients to fulfill it," Enrique answered, siding emphatically with Joanna's observation.

"This whole time I thought I did not go to a university because I was not smart enough or because I did not work hard enough, yet little did I know that I was not given this secret formula or the ingredients! Now I have to go to community college. Who knows if I will ever make it out?" Mayra remarked unhappily as she smacked her lips while in her own class notes she drew a Frida Kahlo-inspired watermelon with "*Viva Los De Oxnard*" carved in it.

Many of her classmates also nodded in agreement as they, too, thought the same about their college-going aspirations.

Mr. Blanch remained quiet and ashamed—he was naively unaware of these injustices. He became upset at himself for taking part in them. Like Mayra and most of her classmates, Mr. Blanch thought his students did not go to four-year universities because they were not good enough. Very few had any talent, or so he thought. After all, they are from Oxnard, how much talent could there possibly be, he wondered? But after being schooled by Enrique, he reconsidered his stance. Perhaps, he pondered, the real reason why his students don't go to universities is because of the lack of formula and ingredients—both of which implicitly tell all Oxnard students they are not meant to go to four-year universities.

Because of all the commotion, confusion, anger, and important information, the 50-minute class flew by without notice. As it always seemed to be the case, Mr. Blanch was saved by the bell, literally. Immediately after the bell rang, students exited his classroom slowly as they dogged him out in disgust and shook their heads.

"Highly Inconsiderate Tests"

You have 45 minutes remaining to complete the test

45 minutes remaining until the test is done
45 minutes to determine whether someone is smart or dumb

45 minutes until this test is used to evaluate whether a teacher is efficient
45 minutes until another student is considered academically deficient

"Highly Inconsiderate Tests"

You have 30 minutes remaining to complete the test

30 minutes to keep those who may not be as fortuitous and privileged behind
30 minutes to confirm that this test was not designed with marginalized people in mind

You have 20 minutes remaining to complete the test

20 minutes to recount notes and lectures in order to successfully pass
20 minutes left of this test that measures exposure to the values and experiences of the white middle class

20 minutes to figure out what chandelier means and entails
20 minutes until someone who has never been exposed to a fancy light fails

You have 10 minutes remaining to complete the test

10 minutes until someone's true abilities and capabilities are not exemplified
10 minutes until someone who has many other strengths and assets is denied

10 minutes that will not assess toughness or resiliency
10 minutes that measures success with very little validity

You have 5 minutes remaining to complete the test

5 minutes of this test that consists of what may appear to be as
irrelevant information
5 minutes until the results of this test encourage alienation

5 minutes left to blame a student for not learning in class
5 minutes remain of a test that completely disregards that
some students are working-class

You have 3 minutes remaining to complete the test

3 minutes and yet some people claim this test is a fair and
neutral tool
3 minutes until someone is out of luck to get into his/her
dream school

You have 1 minute remaining to complete the test

1 minute remains to guess and hope for the best
1 minute until someone's future is determined by this test

The test is now over. Please put your pencil down.

Where is Michele Serros?

I did not know people who looked like me, much less from Oxnard, could write books or create nationally recognized poetry. But then again, I am a victim of what educators call a culturally irrelevant curriculum. This means that most of what I read in the schools I attended did not resonate with my life experiences, nor did educators teach me in an engaging way. In other words, I was deprived. In very little of what I read and saw in schools, did anyone looked like me, spoke like me, and thought like me. Hardly did the curriculum ever speak directly to my cultural identity or my everyday experiences.

2,500 miles away from home, across the country at a predominantly white university in upstate New York, I came across Michele Serros' work. To be candid, this was the last place I would imagine being introduced to her. I have been in school for more than 18 years and I have never read nor seen her work, let alone heard of her. I first listened to her humorous, yet serious poem "Attention Shoppers" in my second year of graduate school. It was too late to actually meet her or send her an email as she had passed away just the year prior. Nonetheless, she read the poem to me, well, virtually at least. My professor, a Mexican American from Riverside, CA, played the poem off her CD, *Chicana Falsa*, and so I heard her voice. He played it at the beginning of class to introduce us to different ways of thinking and writing, period. Serros inspired him to think critically about social injustices through poetry and storytelling when he was in graduate school, so he wanted her to do the same for us.

After class ended, I looked her up to find out more information about her since I really enjoyed her poem. To my surprise, she was born and raised in Oxnard, specifically El Rio. I couldn't believe it. She couldn't possibly be born in El Rio! They don't teach you to read or write in El Rio, or anywhere in Oxnard for that matter! El Rio doesn't even have cement sidewalks! It's all dirt, so your shoes get all messed up! That's one of the reasons why I wouldn't visit my *tío* who lives there. This couldn't be true. But it was! Serros was a Latina, better yet a Chicana, although she wrote about being labeled as a false one. She was also a first-generation college student. Nevertheless, she was a Mexican from Oxnard and she had made it. While she was only a community college student, her first book of poetry and short stories, *Chicana Falsa and other stories of Death, Identity and Oxnard*, was published in 1994. Equally impressive, Serros was chosen as one of 12 poets to tour with Lollapalooza, a well-known annual music festival featuring popular alternative rock, heavy metal, punk rock, hip hop, and EDM bands and artists, dance and comedy performances, and craft booths. I didn't even know poets were invited to this music festival. But there she was, someone from Oxnard breaking barriers.

Having been raised in Oxnard, all of Serros' accomplishments and successes made me proud to be from a city that is often associated with negativity, especially gangs and violence. As soon as I found out she was from Oxnard, I sent some of my friends her poems and told them to look her up. National Public Radio (NPR) did a special on her after her death and I shared that link via text message to everyone I knew. I downloaded her CD, made copies, and uploaded it to a Google drive in order to share her work that way, too. I even sent her work to my friends who were not from Oxnard to let them know that's how we do it where I am from. Not surprisingly, most of her work resonated with me in one way or another. She has a poem in which she talks about how her dad equated "good" parking with "free" parking. Similarly, my family would show up early to an event in order to find "good" parking. Just listening to her voice reminded me of home. Even though I have only known about her for a little under three years, she is an inspiration to me. I laughed at all her funny and creative stories, which were nothing like I have ever heard, seen, or read before.

While I was beyond delighted to have come across Serros' work, I was disappointed it came at such a late stage of my education. Had I known about her work earlier in my childhood years or even in high school, the thought of writing a book or attending a university and making an impact on others' lives would not have seemed as a far-fetched, unattainable endeavor. Instead, some of the readings I remember in class did not remotely relate to my own experiences. For instance, we read *Macbeth*, a story about a Scottish soldier who is predicted to be king, or *Lord of the Flies*, a story about a group of *British* boys stuck on an uninhabited island who try to govern themselves with disastrous results. For reals? What does a Scottish soldier have to do with my life? Where was Michele Serros' work then?

In hindsight, I think about how I could possibly engage in material that was so foreign and irrelevant not only to what I was going through at that moment in my life, but also to what I have observed and experienced growing up. It is no wonder why my high school has horrible college-going rates. The curriculum is culturally irrelevant and absolutely unresponsive to our interests and needs. Why would we want to continue to college or university, if we do not have a meaningful relationship to school?

In a university course that I teach to future educators, I

speak frequently about the importance of tailoring curriculum to the lives and experiences of the students they are teaching. Of course, this is easier said than done. However, it has been done successfully. I share successful examples with my students and remind them constantly of how possible it is. For example, we watch, *Precious Knowledge*, which is a documentary centered on the banning of the Mexican American Studies Program in the Tucson Unified School District of Arizona. This film documents and illustrates how influential, powerful, and effective the Mexican American Studies Program was. This documentary also underscores how the curriculum itself, if culturally responsive, engages the students in ways they have never been engaged before and challenges them to strive to not only graduate high school, but also pursue higher education and critically question their social positions.

Another example I share has to do with Jonathan Kozol. Kozol, an older white man, was fired for teaching a Langston Hughes poem at a predominantly Black school. He was assigned a "bad" fourth grade class, some of who could barely read or write. He wanted to keep them entertained and engaged, so he read poems that spoke to their lived realities. He read Hughes's "The Ballad of the Landlord," which spoke about paying rent and bad living conditions. Through teaching Langston Hughes, he tried to get them to want to read, as it was clear to him that they weren't interested in the textbooks the school had initially assigned for them to read. I share the example of Kozol because he had the courage and insight to deviate from the assigned curriculum to a more appealing one for students who seemed to be disengaged with the material.

Whenever I visit Oxnard schools to speak about higher education, some students immediately tell me that they are not going to college because school is not for them. Their negative experiences with school have gotten in the way of their education. I strongly believe that having a curriculum that reflects students' backgrounds and interests creates a drastically different relationship to learning and schooling. If students feel as if what they are learning in school resonates with their realities, then they would look forward to coming to school every day. Unfortunately, this is not the case. Then we wonder why students with marginalized identities dread going to school. They hardly read or see anything that represents them, and are seldom introduced to anything that cultivates a better understanding of their social position and cultural identities. In many cases, the teachers themselves do not reflect anything about the students they teach nor can they relate to their students on a personal level.

The absence of a culturally relevant curriculum suggests that the students' lived realities and experiences are not important nor in need of stimulation. Introducing Oxnard students to authors such as Serros or others who look and sound like them at a young age could inspire them to have a transformative relationship with school and education. That is, a relationship that encourages them to continue with school past high school. More importantly, one that transforms their perception that school is not meant for them.

Siguiendo Adelante

On a late evening in the fall, the city of Oxnard hosted a citywide town hall meeting on parent involvement and education. Because this meeting started late at night, it gave parents enough time to get out of work, so a lot of Oxnard residents were in attendance. This included caring moms, impatient dads, *chismosas/sos tías y tíos*, barely-walking grandparents and babies, students in all grade levels including college students and graduates, teachers, administrators, and so on—even some family *perritos* made it to the meeting.

Many attendees were Spanish-only speakers, but fortunately, Ms. Solis volunteered to serve as the translator. As many people at this assembly already knew, Oxnard schools have historically performed horribly academically. School personnel insisted the reasons are due to parents not being as involved with nor caring about their children's education as much as they should.

At this overfilled and extremely stuffy town hall meeting, it became obvious that poor Mexican parents in Oxnard were not allowed to value their children's education. This is mainly because there was a set expectation as to what it means to value education. This set expectation excluded and straight up neglected the actions and gestures performed by many poor Mexican parents on a daily basis. These parents had and will continue to have many aspirations and endeavors in mind for their children, yet they are unsure whether their children will pursue them. To be sure, they raised concerns, but given their language barriers, these concerns were overlooked, if not completely unacknowledged. Indeed, they were constantly misunderstood as not caring for their children's education.

A little after 8pm, the school district superintendent, Monica Rodriguez, quieted the crowd by using the "clap if you can hear me" exercise. As soon as the crowd quieted, she began the town hall meeting.

"Hi everyone. Thank you for coming out to this very important meeting about your children's education," Mrs. Rodriguez welcomed the crowd.

105

Mrs. Rodriguez then shared examples of Scott's parents' educational involvement, which she believed everyone should strive for. Scott's family lived in Victoria Estates, a gated, wealthier community in Oxnard. His family has some serious money. His parents and three older siblings all went to college. His dad was white and his mom was third-generation Mexican. Anyways, Scott consistently made honor roll every other semester, so it is automatically presumed that his parents must have been doing something right.

She continued in a somber tone, "We recently received our latest report on our students' evaluations. Unfortunately, we continue to have extremely low scores. Us, as school personnel, are doing what we are supposed to do on our end. However, despite our strenuous efforts, we cannot do it all. We ask that you as parents also contribute on your end. For example, we all need to aspire to be like Scott's parents. Scott was assigned a school project on the Alcatraz prison, which is located in the Bay Area in Northern California. His parents, Mayra and Kurt, drove six and a half hours to ensure that their child got an in-person visual along with detailed information tour about the prison, which is now a museum," Mrs. Rodriguez said as she smiled innocently toward the crowd.

"Needless to say, Scott received an A+. As a matter of fact, he was even nominated for an award for this project, which resulted in him getting a $50 gift card to the local mall." Ms. Solis translated and a handful of members in the crowd reluctantly clapped while also revealing you-think-you-are-all-bad smirks on their faces.

It became obvious that after these comments were made, attendees immediately began to internalize this belief that they *did not* value their children's education to the extent as other parents such as Scott's because they were not as involved. Many faces in audience turned red out of embarrassment and their bodies drooped as if they had just dropped their *mango con chile paletas*.

Materially speaking, it was merely impossible for these poor Mexican parents to provide as much as Scott's parents. Many of them could barely afford rent and bills. By this same twisted logic, how could they as parents possibly begin to value their children's education if they have very little resources to help supplement it? This thought ran through their minds. Some, but not all of them, were in agreement with the idea that valuing education is highly if not solely correlated with materialism. In other words, there were more than a handful of people in the crowd who saw valuing an education as providing tutoring services to their child who needed additional educational services.

Like the school superintendent, they found themselves comparing, if not competing, with classmates and friends' educational support such as Scott's parents. Such comparison never took into consideration the drastic differences in household incomes, even though that was an important and relevant factor. Also, this comparison hid the fact that many parents were not formally educated in their home countries, much less in the U.S. Thus, they were unfamiliar with how this particular educational system works. To be sure, they

107

believed dearly in the idea that when it comes to education, there is a level playing field.

A long and shameful minute passed after Mrs. Rodriguez's remarks about Scott's parents. There would have been cricket sounds had it not been for the crying babies in the hot and stuffy auditorium.

Micaela, a recent college graduate who was just accepted to graduate school, slowly raised her hand, "With all due respect Mrs. Rodriguez, but you can't possibly expect our parents to replicate Scott's parents' educational involvement. Not only do my parents not have the privilege of taking off days from work to casually take me to a museum, but also my parents can't even afford a reliable car. Shoot! We would barely make it to the freeway," the crowd giggled at her sarcasm.

"That's right, *Mija*," her *Tío Antonio* shouted, echoing his voice with his hands shaped as a megaphone.

Dr. Emmanuel Lopez, who grew up in Oxnard and is now a professor at a nearby university, contributed, "Micaela has a really good point. We as a society are extremely infatuated with dominant notions of what it means to value education. For example, parents are expected to automatically help their children with their homework. However, this assumes that all parents have the same or a similar educational background, which is not always the case. These comparisons are not fair and they do more harm than good."

He grasped for air, repeated what he said in Spanish to give Ms. Solis a break, looked at the crowd who was patiently looking back at him, and then continued, "In fact, for the seminar I teach in graduate school, the first book I assign is *The Education of Blacks in the South, 1860-1935* by historian James Anderson. In this book, Anderson puts forth compelling examples that challenge the narrative that the main reason why Blacks are not successful academically is because they do not value education nor have ever valued it. Anderson suggests otherwise in that Blacks exchanged their cattle in return for materials to build schoolhouses. They even volunteered their own time in hard manual labor by carrying heavy logs to help build schools. These actions are nontraditional ways of valuing education. Y'all get me?"

Members in the crowd nodded in agreement and filled the auditorium with loud claps and shouts.

Emilio, a freshman at a local high school, interjected shyly, "Yeah, that makes sense. My mom tries to help me with whatever ways possible. Once I was given a memorable and dreadful homework assignment for being a so-called 'class clown.' This was no ordinary homework. This assignment was absolutely pointless. Like Bart Simpson in the opening credits of *The Simpsons*, I was required to write down a phrase that spoke directly to what I had done wrong in class X amount of times. I explained this situation to my mom and she agreed that this was a pointless assignment, yet she also acknowledged that it was important for me to complete and turn in on time before I was penalized even more. Given the language barrier and my mom's low levels of education, I hardly asked her for academic assistance. Long story short, my mom insisted that she needed to help me. Despite having very little education, my mom assisted me in whatever ways she could, this instance being one of many. To me, my mother was aware of the importance of completing and turning in any assignment, regardless of how ridiculous it may be, on time in order to avoid any further penalties and that's why she helped me." Following Emilio's testimony, a round of applause erupted throughout the audience to recognize his courage to share his story.

Angelica, Emilio's mom who was proudly sitting next to him, added in Spanish, "Yes, very true *Mijo*. I remember that day. We even convinced your brother's best friend, Pete, to help us, too. While I worked on one page, you and Pete worked on the others. Together we managed to get the assignment done before the night ended. Late at night, mind you, but we got it done. Three distinct handwritings and all, but it was complete. To Emilio's point, Pete, who helped us, did not complete high school and was often labeled as a gang member. I am confident to think that he helped us because he too understood the importance of completing assignments so that Emilio would be given educational opportunities he was unable to take advantage of."

At this point the audience members began to talk among each other recounting various ways they, too, valued their children's education. Still, no one volunteered to say anything aloud.

As soon as the crowd settled down, José, a senior in high school, then shared his experience, "My parents cared about

110

my education, too!" he exclaimed. "Of course, it looked a little differently since we are poor. When I did not get good grades, I did not get a tutor. Instead, I got an ass whooping."

The crowd chuckled uncontrollably at his joke.

"*La chancla* helps grades, *tambien*!" an *abuelita* sitting in the front row yelled while gasping for air.

José smiled, "In my opinion, my parents showed that they cared that I did well in school; however, because we couldn't afford to hire a tutor, they used whatever means they had to make sure I knew the importance of an education. I would argue that even if my parents could afford a tutor, they might not have hired one. Again, not because they do not care about my education, but because they assumed tutors are provided by the school."

"As they should be!" Ms. Jimenez, a local activist and mother, shouted at the top of her lungs from the back of the room.

"My parents sacrificed a lot for my education, too" Esmeralda protested. "Like many of us here, my parents do not have a lot of money or resources. Still, I am finishing my third year at a university."

Chifles and shouts came from the crowd as if she had just graduated from middle school all over again.

"Despite these drastic differences in household incomes between myself and my classmates, my parents performed actions that contributed tremendously to my education. Whenever I went home, my parents wondered how I was doing financially. Because of their financial constraints and

111

struggles, they could not support me financially and I am okay with that. Even though I was the first to attend college, it became obvious that my family understood the notion of a struggling college student. Whenever they were in need of money, I was the last person they asked. They felt guilty when they asked me for money because they weren't giving me any in return to help my studies. Both of my parents would say, *'Esa niña es para que le demos, no para que le quitemos.'* This literally translates to, 'We should be giving, not taking from that kid.' To me, this translates to, it's bad enough we do not have anything to offer, why should we take anything away from her. By not asking me for money in times of need, their message shows me that they wanted me to continue studying without any interruptions."

Immediately after her statement, tears of both sadness and pride ran down her cheeks.

"I have a similar story," nodded Alfredo as he hugged his mom.

"In high school, my mother made a generous deal with me regarding her one and only car. Despite the fact that my mom only had one car, she told me she would let me drive the car to school every Tuesday and Thursday if I promised her that I would do the following two things. One, I actually need to go to school and not ditch or leave school early; and two, not only do I need to go, but I also have to do well in school. Since it was considered 'cool' to drive to high school, I took my mom's offer very seriously and made sure I did everything I needed to in order to drive to school.

Consequently, this meant that every Tuesday and Thursday my mom would have to struggle to find her way to wherever she needed to go during those two days. Yet, even though my mom knew her car would be parked in the school's parking lot practically all day, not being put to use, she really wanted me to do well in school, so it was worth the hassle. In my opinion, since my mother could not afford to bribe me with money to do well in school as some parents do, she used the very little resources she had—her only car—to incentivize education."

Alfredo continued, "Similarly, even though there was a school bus stop right around the corner of my house, my mom understood I was embarrassed to take it and she would never hesitate to take me to school when I would ask her to on the days that I did not drive myself. Like many of us, I paid little attention to the subtle, yet important ways my mother supported my education. Minor actions such as letting me take the car to school or giving me a ride instead of forcing me to take the bus, further underscore some of the ways my mother not only contributed to, but also invested in my education."

"As a Madre, I can attest to some of these sacrifices personally," Señora Villanueva, a local Madre of three, stated in a firm tone while pointing directly at the school superintendent.

"Since I live by one of the 'best' schools in Oxnard, which offers bilingual classes to students by the way, I am frequently asked the following question by friends, relatives, and even strangers, '*¡Oye! ¿Me prestas tu dirección de correo?*' Initially, I always wondered why some parents—sometimes even my own relatives—would ask if they could use someone else's mailing address for school purposes? Now, the explanation is clear to me. Since schools require parents to enroll their children according to where they reside, parents try to find ways to avoid sending their children to schools that they perceive to be not as good as others."

"*¡Y sí! ¡Asi es la cosa!*" another *Madre* yelled from the background.

Señora Villanueva continued, "That being said, I strongly believe that these parents knew that using someone else's mailing address for school purposes was only part of the equation. The other part had to do with getting their kids to school. When these Mexican parents asked to use my mailing address, they not only sought to enroll their child in a better school, but practically agreed that they are more than willing to find a way to get their child to school every single day, despite the length and time of a commute. I know some of these parents personally and they live very far from my home. The commute to school would be nothing less than troublesome, yet they pleaded for such request, regardless of what they had to go through. The process, including humiliation and nerves, that these Mexican parents have to go through further exemplifies their persistence and commitment for better schooling for their children. Now that right there is dedication for better schooling!"

Again, the crowd mumbled in anger because they, too, have similar stories in which despite having very little resources, they performed various actions and assisted their children in many ways that contributed positively to their children's educational experiences.

Mrs. Rodriguez patiently calmed the crowd down by thanking them for their thoughtful responses.

Lorena, a mother of two and local activist, suggested the following, "Mrs. Rodriguez, we really appreciate your concern about our students. As you can tell by the attendance of this town hall, we are very concerned, too. However, we want to you pay close attention to various ways these parents care deeply about their children's education. Your explanation as to why our children are not doing well in school personifies a cultural deficit outlook. This outlook immediately blames the kids and their family's culture. For example, it assumes that Mexican parents do not care about their children's education because they do not show up for teacher-parent conferences."

"That's true! I don't go because the school never provides translation services and because they are scheduled at inconvenient times for me," Señora Chavira declared unapologetically in Spanish.

"You see," Lorena faced the crowd with her arms spread out like a priest during Mass.

"We care, but our efforts and concerns are downplayed or unacknowledged. As a whole, we need to give credit when credit is due. We have to pay attention to the various everyday actions, duties, and roles that us, as poor Mexican parents, perform that unquestionably emphasize the importance of an education. Simply because some of us cannot afford to send their children to college or are not familiar with what it takes to get to college, does not mean that we do not value education. It certainly doesn't mean we get blamed for it! To use the example that Professor Lopez introduced us to, I am more than convinced that all the parents in this room have traded what would be equivalent to their cattle in exchange for a better education for their children. *¡A que seguir adelante!*"

* *Dedicado a mis padres,* María *y* Pablo

Athletic Scholie

"Sonia! Hurry up and turn on the TV! I want to see if Oxnard High's football team beat Channel Islands," Eduardo yelled as he walked down the stairs to the living room.

"Chill! You know they always do, but anyways, it's already on," Sonia responded and changed the TV to Channel 3.

As soon as Eduardo made himself comfortable in his mom's rocking chair, his eyes were immediately glued to the TV.

"Hello, this is Ron Johnson, thank you for tuning into Friday Night Lights—dedicated to providing you updates and scores of your local schools' sports teams. There have been many accomplishments this week. Alison Dale, a senior at Leadership High School in Westlake, California, has received a full athletic scholarship to be a part of Washington State University's women's rowing team as their designated coxswain. Alison is following the steps of her older sister, Morgan, who is already on Washington State's rowing team."

"Yo, what in the heck is a cocks-wang?" Eduardo asked while raising his eyebrows.

Sonia, already on her phone, muted the TV and then proceeded to look it up on Google, "How do you spell it?"

"Ummm. Type 'rowing,' then c-o-c-k-s-w-a-n-g," Eduardo laughed out loud knowing he just guessed horribly.

"Homie, you were way off! It's c-o-x-s-w-a-i-n," Sonia struggled trying to spell it out. "According to Google, a coxswain is the person who sits in the front of the boat facing the other rowers and verbally and physically controls the boat's steering, speed, timing and fluidity. It says here that the coxswain is constantly yelling commands at other rowers in the same boat."

"You gotta be kidding me! People get athletic scholies for yelling at other people?! Yo! Moms could have gone to Harvard!" Eduardo suggested quietly so that his mom in the other room didn't hear him.

Sonia laughed and then insisted matter-of-factly, "Not just ordinary people, but people who can afford boats and training for those boats! When was the last time you were on a boat?"

"Dang! When we went to Six Flags. Remember? The one that makes your stomach feel all weird," Eduardo smirked jokingly.

"Not that kind of boat, foo!" Sonia responded by throwing a pillow at him.

Eduardo threw the pillow back, "Even though we live so close to the beach, I don't think I know anyone in Oxnard who owns a boat, much less a rowing boat. Now that I think about it, Oxnard High doesn't even have a rowing team! We barely have a pool for water polo and swimming. And I think we share it with other high schools! Shake my head!"

He continued, "Had I known I could have gotten an athletic scholie for yelling at people on the rowing team, I would have been preparing my lungs! But since we don't even have a rowing team, I didn't even get a chance at that scholie. Yo! That's messed up!" Eduardo exclaimed as he smacked his lips and shook his head.

"That's why I always tell you, focus on your grades and get an 'academic scholie.' Those exist, too, in case you didn't know. And you do not have to yell at anybody. Well, maybe if that financial aid check doesn't come in on time," Sonia replied in a semi-serious tone.

Eduardo stared at the TV for a good minute. "Dang. I'm still thinking about this cocks-wang and sports in general. I didn't even think athletic scholies could be so exclusionary like that. I thought it was all about talent or hard work ethic."

119

"Clearly not," Sonia responded immediately.

"Hold up," Eduardo paused as if he just had an epiphany. "Remember when Dad took us to the NCAA Division 1 Men's soccer tournament in LA?" Eduardo asked excitedly.

"Yeah, what about it?" Sonia answered, quick as a flash without any emotion.

"Correct me if I am wrong, but from what I remember, almost all the players on those Division 1 university soccer teams were white. Some were even from white European countries like Germany or Italy. Sure, there were a few domestic Brown and Black players here and there, but almost all of them were mostly white, remember?" Eduardo asserted cleverly.

"Yeah, they were. And? What's your point?" Sonia said not persuaded by his point.

"It doesn't make sense to me," Eduardo whispered in a confused manner. "Oxnard has a lot of talented soccer players. My senior year in high school, the CIF championship was between two Oxnard high schools! My high school could have made it, too, but we were disqualified. That's another story for another day. Anyhow, every other year, an Oxnard high school soccer team is a runner up for the CIF championship. I am telling you, soccer runs in our bloods. So much freaking soccer talent in Oxnard."

"Let's not forget about the Oxnard girls! Recently, the Oxnard girls' soccer team won the CIF championship, too!" Sonia interjected proudly while looking at her phone.

"Yup! Them too! Besides having all these champions and talented soccer players, I never see any of them go on to play for championships at the NCAA Division 1 soccer tournament. I am thinking there is some type of exclusion here. Even in soccer we are excluded."

"Yeah, it's because we are Mexican!" Sonia said sarcastically.

"You say that for everything! I am being serious. I rarely see anyone from Oxnard play soccer for UCLA. We saw them play at that tournament when dad took us. No disrespect, but they were trash! Remember Roberto from my high school team?" Eduardo asked.

"The one with the messed-up blonde-ish haircut?" Sonia responded.

"Yeah," he laughed. "That foo was good enough and could have made the UCLA squad easily. He was the leading scorer in our high school league for four years. Even as a freshman he led the league in scoring! But once again we weren't given that opportunity."

"Besides 'so-called' soccer-talent, what else do these preppy white kids have that we don't in Oxnard? In regards to rowing, it is easy. They have boats and we don't. But when it comes to soccer, we have fields and balls. So what is it?" Eduardo nagged aloud.

"Well, they are called 'student-athletes' for a reason. We might have lots of athletes and talent, but we certainly don't have enough students. You know Oxnard schools don't

121

prepare us for college! That's one thing for sure," Sonia suggested.

She continued, "Come to think about it, I had a class with a Division 1 basketball athlete in college and he told me that there is a science to being recruited for all university sports teams. One thing I remember him saying is that you must play in private tournaments outside of your school's season to gain exposure to college coaches."

"Dang! Remember why I had to quit the LA Waves soccer travel team?" Eduardo complained.

"Yup! It was half our rent just to get to practice from Oxnard to LA," Sonia recalled.

"You see, I told dad it was a good investment. I would have been playing D-1 soccer!" Eduardo said proudly.

"Yeah right! You sleeping in the dorms while we wouldn't have a home." Sonia continued, "He also said that you need an extensive highlight reel—one that shows your different skills and strengths. To that, he even said, depending on school or coach, the music someone includes in this highlight reel makes or breaks the scholarship! It is that specific! Some of your homies had Lil Wayne on their basketball highlight tapes. Laugh out loud. You know they didn't get looked at by prestigious universities," she said while laughing at her own joke.

"That's it!" Eduardo shouted as he jumped out of his seat. He pulled out his phone out of his pocket and called his friend, Emmanuel, who was the captain and goalie of his high school soccer team.

After the short phone call, he told Sonia, "Emmanuel said that we didn't even have someone consistently recording us while we played. He said some games we did, but other games we did not. It was so unorganized. How should we even expect to be recruited for D-1 universities if we can't even send them a highlight tape? Our schools barely bought us uniforms, what makes you think they are going to buy us top notch videotaping materials or video editing software," Eduardo protested.

"That's so dumb! We have so much potential, but it cannot be fulfilled. Not even in sports!" Eduardo said in a frustrated tone.

"Those are just two ways poor Brown and Black people from Oxnard are excluded from athletic scholarships. Depending on the sport, I am sure there are a lot more ways we get excluded from athletic scholarships," Sonia reminded him.

"I guess the rapper *Jadakiss* wasn't lying when he asked us to think about why the brother up north better than Jordan didn't get that break?" Eduardo thought to himself quietly as they continued to watch the local sports highlights.

"Look! The scores are on!" Sonia unmuted the TV.

"This is Ron Johnson again, Oxnard High beats Channel Islands for the fourth year in a row . . ."

Fresas y Mentiras

Oxnard is surrounded by all kinds of agricultural fields that yield various crops from lima beans to sugar beets, but most notably *fresas*. To be specific, Oxnard is the "home of *las fresas*." It is without a doubt one of the largest strawberry growers in the nation. In fact, every year the city hosts the California Strawberry Festival, where you will find strawberry everything—strawberry nachos, strawberry pizza, or even, if you're old enough, strawberry champagne.

Griselda's first time at the strawberry festival in Oxnard was one for the books. Despite being born and raised in Oxnard for 14 years, she had never gone. Actually, because it was hella expensive, almost all her friends and relatives had never been there either. Anyways, her first visit was memorable, but not because she finally got to try the world famous strawberry salsa or the perfectly dipped and freshly picked chocolate-covered strawberries. No, nothing like that. She went strictly for business. It was an extra credit opportunity she was given to make up for how horribly she did on her English paper earlier in her summer school session. She knew she had to pass her summer session English class, so she took advantage of an extra-credit opportunity to do a research project of her own interest.

Both of Griselda's parents are agricultural workers, so she decided to do her project on *fresas*—something she was extremely interested in because of her parents' work experiences. Her teacher, Mr. García, had suggested that she check out the timely strawberry festival to supplement her interviews she conducted with her parents. He even paid for her admission ticket. He was always a supportive and thoughtful teacher who would go out of his way to make sure his students were engaged in his class. The flexibility of this assignment is a prime example of how he would make students itch for an education. So that's how Griselda ended up at the California Strawberry Festival for her first and soon-to-be last time.

Throughout the short span of her research project, Griselda immediately noticed a drastic disjuncture between the responses she gathered through the interviews she conducted with her parents and what she saw at the strawberry festival. For example, an obvious difference was that everything at the strawberry festival was so happy and joyful. This didn't make sense to Griselda because everything her parents had told her about picking strawberries was disheartening and infuriating. From what she observed growing up, strawberry picking was no joke. Still, people from all over the nation would come to celebrate and praise a *fruta*. But these same people would pay no mind to those who picked it. It was as if the pickers themselves neither existed nor mattered.

As one would dare to imagine, the life of undocumented agricultural workers is a tough one, to say the least. In sum, Griselda's parents' responses varied from working long shifts with very few breaks or none at all, to being denied workers' compensation for their work-related injuries. Her dad even broke down crying when he shared his experiences of being paid low wages and about the many times when he was not paid at all. Griselda remembered when this happened because she came home to a house full of lit candles because her parents couldn't afford the electricity bill.

None of the injustices underscored by her parents were remotely talked about or even mentioned at the California Strawberry Festival in Oxnard. It was filled with *mentiras*. These fancy schmancy festivalgoers were completely oblivious to or in denial of the strawberry-picking process. They acted as if these strawberries just magically appeared. To Griselda, these people who paid the overpriced $12 admission fee were being deceived and lied to. They were only being told one side of the story, which focused on the end product—*las fresas*. However, this side of the story was glorified and romanticized. People at this festival were not being exposed to the ugly, hidden truth; that is, the unethical hardships that come along with being an undocumented agricultural worker like her parents. Something she was too familiar with and thought was important to address and bring to the forefront, especially at a festival about *fresas*.

Along these lines, this research project also served as a way for Griselda to reflect on other *mentiras* she had been told all her life. For as long as she could remember, everyone, including her own parents, has constantly told her that if she works hard then she will be rewarded. To be sure, her research project has also encouraged her to disrupt this notion that our society is based on merit. People call it meritocracy, or the "American Dream" or the "*solo se necesitan ganas*." Supposedly, success in the U.S. is based on merit or hard work. Yet this runs contrary to what she learned from her research project and from what she observed growing up as a child of undocumented Mexican immigrants.

Strawberry picking is all about working hard. As a matter of fact, strawberry pickers don't get paid by the hour. As piecemeal workers, they get paid for as many baskets of strawberries they can fill; therefore, it behooves them to work as hard as possible to make as much as possible. So, in other words, they *should* get paid by how hard they work. But, because these workers only get some cents for every basket they fill, Griselda found that strawberry pickers would be lucky if they made $4 an hour. And since most of the strawberry pickers she knows are undocumented, they are unable to get another job and are afraid to file complaints because it increases the risks of being deported.

To this, Griselda's research paper argued that strawberry picking as a profession completely challenges the idea if someone works hard, then they will be rewarded. Her parents wake up at 4:00am to get to work on time at 5:00am and they work until 4:30pm, some days even longer. Frequently, her parents beat the sun going up and return home when the sun is going down. Though they are some of the hardest working people in Oxnard, they still remain poor. They haven't been rewarded and Griselda doubts they ever will.

After completing her project, Griselda presented her research findings at the city council meeting in Oxnard. She also wrote a letter to the Mayor of Oxnard requesting an increase of awareness and actions concerning the harsh working conditions of agricultural workers in Oxnard. Still, three years later, she hasn't seen much change. Ultimately, this research project has reminded and encouraged Griselda about the importance of humanizing agricultural workers. Because many of them are undocumented and do not have rights, they are treated as if they are not humans—often referred to as "aliens" as if they drove space ships or something. How silly and messed up is that?

Now, whenever she rides in the raggedy, bright yellow school bus down Victoria Avenue to her high school, another place filed with *mentiras*, Griselda makes it a priority to look out of the window onto the back-bent-over strawberry pickers. She does this to pay respect to her parents, as well as all the other field workers who toil tirelessly but are not being rewarded nor treated as humans. That being said, next time you bite into a perfectly ripe Oxnard-grown *fresa,* or any other crop from anywhere for that matter, you must pay homage to the exploited agricultural workers who made it possible for you to enjoy it.

35¢ Sodas

A dollar used to go a long way in Oxnard. In some areas, it still does. It's mostly in the Southside, though. Usually, the closer you get to the beach, the more your dollar shrinks. Things are changing, so even as you get farther from the beach, prices continue to rise, too. Needless to say, I never thought I'd grow old enough to use the phrase, "Back in my day, a dollar would buy me so much." Growing up in the Blue Ghetto, a congested, low-income condominium community that separates Port Hueneme from Oxnard, we would cross the street to buy amenities and use services from the run-down shopping plaza off Victoria Ave and Hemlock Street. Even though we never called it by its official name, word on the street is that the name of this shopping plaza was the "Channel Islands Shopping Center."

Despite having a beat-up parking lot and excessive, scary empty storefronts, including a seemingly haunted Albertsons grocery store with broken windows, residents of the Blue Ghetto and nearby neighbors utilized this shopping plaza. Whenever my mom would have to wash our blankets or other large loads, we would go to the *lavanderia* at this location. It was practically the same price as our condo complex, but since the washing and drying machines were much bigger, we would get our money's worth.

The donut shop always came in clutch in the mornings, afternoons, and evenings. You couldn't go wrong with any of the 75¢ donuts. My go-to donut was the one with a chocolate chip outer layer and a chocolate chip fill-in. Of course, this one just happened to be the most expensive, costing a whopping $1.50. If you played your cards right, though, you could enjoy your donut with a movie rental from the fake Blockbuster spot next door for no more than $4. Better yet, if you felt like treating yourself, you could upgrade your donut for a pulled pork sandwich at the BBQ joint on the other side of the video store. I always thought it was funny that they would BBQ in the middle of the empty parking lot so the smoke wouldn't be bothersome, but that's another story for another day.

131

Aside from the grub and entertainment, this plaza also offered two means to keep you semi-fresh. The first was a thrift store, which is why I said *semi*-fresh. This was always a hit or miss. Depending on the batch of clothes and accessories, you may be able to find yourself a nice outfit, and on certain days, you even got a discount on the different colored tags. The second was the barbershop where I was a regular. This was mostly because I had to keep my double line-up fresh. The owner of the shop would always hook me up, both literally and figuratively. He knew me personally and gave me a discount because I would accompany my friends to the same church he attended.

Out of all the seven or eight spots at this raggedy shopping plaza, the liquor store was my favorite because it was the cheapest—especially compared to the gas station on the other side of the lot that would put happy face stickers over the stamped, suggested retail prices so they could sell their goods for more. At this liquor store, even with only a dollar, the combinations of what to get were endless. The 35¢ Shasta sodas were a local favorite. With so many flavors to choose from, it was so worth it. Grape was always my first pick. If you were thirsty, you could get two sodas and a 30¢ bag of Hot Cheetos. If you were hungry it was vice versa, two bags of Hot Cheetos and one soda. The full course meal included a bag of Hot Cheetos, one soda, and a 35¢ Twinkie for dessert. All for one dollar!

Lots of memories were created at this plaza. Plenty of 35¢ sodas were purchased. Although my friends, *vecinas/os*, and family shopped there and utilized the space, I knew this shopping plaza wouldn't last. In regards to its infrastructure, there wasn't a genuine investment in it. The blacktop was depressingly cracked and the paint on the building walls had faded and peeled. Businesses would have a grand opening one week, only to be followed by a grand closing a few months later. Without the city's help, it was very difficult to maintain a business at this plaza because of how disinvested it looked. After all, who can keep a business viably open next to a haunted grocery store that had been closed for over eight years?

Recently, this plaza was finally demolished. Everything was destroyed. Over the span of a few years, I witnessed half a million dollar townhomes being built in this exact location. Unlike the shopping plaza, former plaza shoppers like myself, my family, or my *vecinas/os* will not utilize these townhomes or even come anywhere near them. The prices of these townhomes are exclusionary in and of themselves. To make matters worse, these *boujee* townhomes already have a lot of surveillance cameras and private property signs reminding us living across the street to stay away.

This is not an isolated incident in Oxnard. It's actually a pattern that I have noticed. Even when there are not signs or cameras explicitly targeting us, poor People of Color are excluded from areas without knowing that we are. A great case in point is the recently built Whole Foods at The Collection. The only People of Color I see there are the workers. Then again, who has money, but more importantly the nerves, to buy $15 organic peanut butter? I know people who work at Whole Foods and still cannot afford to shop there. It's ridiculously expensive, thus exclusionary.

Anyhow, there are different names and ways to explain what happened to the shopping plaza across the street from the Blue Ghetto and to other regions in Oxnard. City officials call it necessary city "revitalization." This means the city finds ways to revive itself by building restaurants or homes that will bring in new people, but more importantly, new money. On another end, city development critics call it "gentrification." This is the process of renovating and improving a city tailored to the tastes of a white middle-class. I call it "no more 35¢ sodas."